CAROL
HIGGINS CLARK

LACED

A Regan Reilly Mystery

Doubleday Large Print
Home Library Edition

SCRIBNER

New York   London   Toronto   Sydney

This Large Print Edition, prepared especially for Double-day Large Print Home Library, contains the complete, unabridged text of the original Publisher's Edition.

SCRIBNER
A Division of Simon & Schuster, Inc.
1230 Avenue of the Americas
New York, NY 10020

Manufactured in the United States of America

ISBN-13: 978-0-7394-8074-8

**This Large Print Book carries the
Seal of Approval of N.A.V.H.**

Acknowledgments

Shamrocks to my editor, Roz Lippel, for all her hard work, advice, encouragement, and friendship. As always, her guidance has been wonderful.

And special thanks to everyone else who saw Regan and Jack Reilly off on their honeymoon to Ireland!

Associate Director of Copyediting Gypsy da Silva, copyeditor Rose Ann Ferrick, and proofreader Barbara Raynor.

Art Director John Fulbrook III, photographer Debra Lill, and photographer Glenn Jussen.

Scribner Publishing Associate, Kara Watson.

My publicist, Lisl Cade.

My agent, Esther Newberg.

My mother, Mary Higgins Clark, my stepfather, John Conheeney, my aunt, Irene Clark, my family and friends.

It's been grand!

In memory of my grandfather,
Luke J. Higgins,
who immigrated to New York from
Ireland as a young man,

And my maternal great-grandparents,
Thomas Durkin and
Bridget Kennedy Durkin,
who came to New York a generation earlier,

And for all my cousins who live
in the Emerald Isle...

With love.

Monday, April 11th

1

In a remote village in the west of Ireland, a light mist rose from the lake behind Hennessy Castle. The afternoon was becoming increasingly gray and brooding as clouds gathered and the skies turned threatening. Inside the castle the fireplaces were lit, providing a cheery warmth for the guests who were already anticipating a wonderful evening meal in the elegant eighteenth-century dining room.

The massive front doors of the castle opened slowly, and newlyweds Regan and Jack Reilly stepped out onto the driveway in their jogging clothes. They'd arrived on an overnight flight from New York, slept for several hours, and decided a quick jog might help alleviate the inevitable jet lag.

Jack looked at his thirty-one-year-old bride, touched her hair, and smiled. "We're in our native land, Mrs. Reilly. Our Irish roots lie before us."

Anyone who saw the handsome couple wouldn't have questioned those roots. Jack was six foot two, with sandy hair, hazel eyes, a firm jaw, and a winning smile. Regan had blue eyes, fair skin, and dark hair—she was one of the black Irish.

"Well, it certainly is green around here," Regan observed as she glanced around at the lush gardens, wooded trails, and rolling lawn. "Everything is so still and quiet."

"After last week, still and quiet sounds good to me," Jack said. "Let's go."

Together they broke into a jog and crossed a pedestrian bridge that traversed a stream in front of the castle. They turned left and headed down an isolated country road that the concierge told them led right into the village. The only sound was their sneakers hitting the pavement. At a curve in the road they passed an old stone church that looked deserted.

Regan pointed toward the steepled building. "I'd love to take a look in there tomorrow."

Jack nodded. "We will." He glanced up at the sky. "I think that rain is coming in faster than we expected. This jog is going to be quick."

But when the road ended at the tiny village, a graveyard with darkened gravestones proved irresistible to Regan. A set of stone steps to their left led up to a courtyard where a broken stone wall surrounded the cemetery. "Jack, let's take a quick look."

"The funeral director's daughter," Jack said affectionately. "You never met a graveyard you didn't like."

Regan smiled. "Those tombstones must be centuries old."

They hurried up the steps, turned right, and stopped in their tracks. The first tombstone they spotted said REILLY.

"This is a good omen," Jack muttered.

Regan leaned forward. "May Reilly. Born in 1760 and died in 1822. There don't seem to be any other Reillys here with her."

"Just as long as there aren't any named Regan or Jack."

Regan was deep in thought. "You know

that joke my father always tells? The one about how an Irishman proposes?"

"You want to be buried with my mother?"

"That's the one. It looks like poor May didn't have anyone, not even a mother-in-law."

"Some people would consider that a good thing." Jack grabbed Regan's hand as large drops of rain started to come down. "Tomorrow we'll spend as much time as you want here figuring out what went wrong in these people's lives. Come on."

Regan smiled. "I can't help it. I'm an investigator."

"So am I."

They didn't encounter a single soul as they ran through the tiny village, which consisted of a pharmacy, two pubs, a souvenir shop, and a butcher. They wound around and jogged back to the castle where they showered and changed.

At 7:30 they went down to dinner and were seated at a table by a large window overlooking the garden. The rain had stopped, and the night was peaceful. Their waiter greeted them warmly.

"Welcome to Hennessy Castle. I trust you're enjoying yourselves so far."

"We certainly are," Regan answered. "But

we stopped by the graveyard in town, and the first tombstone we saw had our name on it."

"Reilly?"

"Yes."

The waiter whistled softly. "You were looking at old May Reilly's grave. She was a talented lacemaker who supposedly haunts the castle, but we haven't heard from her for a while."

"She haunts this place?" Regan asked.

"Apparently May was always complaining that she wasn't appreciated. One of her lace tablecloths is in a display case upstairs in the memorabilia room. She made it for a special banquet of dignitaries who were visiting the Hennessy family, but May got sick and died before they paid her. Legend is that she keeps coming back for her money."

"Sounds like one of my cousins," Jack said.

"I don't blame her," Regan protested. "She should have been paid."

At 4:00 A.M. Regan woke with a start. Jack was sleeping peacefully beside her. The rain had started up again and sounded as if it was coming down harder than before. Regan slipped out of bed and crossed the spacious room to close the window. As she pulled back the curtain, a flash of lightning streaked across the sky. Regan looked down and in the distance saw the figure of a woman dressed in a long black coat, standing on the back lawn in front of the lake. She was staring up at Regan and shaking her fists. One hand was clenching a piece of white material. Could that be lace? Regan wondered.

"Regan, are you all right?" Jack asked.

Regan quickly turned her head away from the window, then just as quickly turned it back. Another bolt of lightning lit up the sky.

The woman was gone.

Jack flicked on the light. "Regan, you look as if you just spotted a ghost."

Before she could answer, the smell of smoke filled their nostrils. A moment later the fire alarm went off.

"So much for peace and quiet," Jack said quickly. "Let's throw on some clothes and get out of here!"

Tuesday, April 12th

2

Regan and Jack had had so many wonderful plans for their honeymoon. Running for their lives down to the somewhat smoky lobby of Hennessy Castle at four in the morning wasn't among them. Their fellow bleary-eyed, agitated travelers were appearing from all directions. Many were in pajamas and robes. Women who at dinner were perfectly made up and coiffed now looked like the "before" picture in beauty magazine makeovers. Regan was glad that she and Jack had quickly thrown on jeans and sweaters and grabbed their jackets.

Life never seems to go the way you plan it,

Regan thought. And I think I just saw a ghost. Married two days. Jack's going to think I'm nuts. But I definitely saw someone, and then she disappeared—which, thankfully, is just what the smoke seems to be doing.

"Just a little grease fire in the kitchen. Thank God no injuries," a sixtyish man wearing a red uniform jacket with gold braiding announced to the crowd. "As you can see, there isn't too much smoke. Although where there's smoke there's fire, I do admit. It's nearly under control. The breakfast cook pulled the fire alarm in a panic. It wasn't really necessary."

A feeling of relief rippled through the crowd.

"My name is Neil Buckley, and I'm the manager of Hennessy Castle. If you don't mind, would you please step outside for a few minutes."

"It's raining!" shouted a woman wearing stiletto shoes and a fluffy feathered pink bathrobe. "If it's under control, we should stay inside!"

"It's a necessary precaution until the firemen give us the okay. Please. Oh—here they are!"

Firemen came rushing through the front door of the castle, lugging their equipment.

"Around the corner to the kitchen!" Buckley cried. "Martin, show them the way if you would!" he ordered a young man who was wearing a red vest with the Hennessy crest.

"Right away, sir!"

The firemen hurried off.

"Now, as I was saying," Buckley continued, "please step outside. The rain is letting up. We have brollies for you by the door."

The pink bathrobed woman pointed her well-manicured hand that was laden with multitiered diamond rings. "We'd better not be charged for tonight!"

Regan shook her head. Just hours ago this castle seemed like a romantic and cozy respite from the crazy fast-paced world. Now an acrid smell hung in the air and one of the seemingly genteel guests was picking a fight about her room charges. Jack put his arm under Regan's elbow, and along with the others, they walked outside onto the dark driveway where it was rainy and chilly.

"Mrs. Reilly, allow me," Jack said with a smile and a raised eyebrow as he started to open their umbrella. But before it was up, a woman who'd been behind them coming out the door became distracted by an impending sneeze. She bumped into Regan as she bellowed *achoo!* Regan was pushed against Jack, which she didn't mind, but she was glad she hadn't ended up on the ground. *"Achoo!"*

Regan and Jack both took a step backward.

"Sorry!" the petite woman said. "Sorry. I'm so allergic to smoke, you can't believe it." She reached in her purse and pulled out a lace handkerchief. "This whole thing is outrageous," she said.

Regan and Jack exchanged a quick smile. "Don't worry about it," Regan said.

The woman, who was probably in her early thirties, was a cute little blond. She couldn't have been more than five foot two. Clutching her white lace handkerchief tightly, she looked as though she were getting ready for the next big *achoo* which was probably on its way. Regan was reminded of the woman she had just seen on the back lawn. She had been clutching something white in her hands, and it seemed natural. But to witness this small woman sneezing like a horse and then dabbing her nose with a dainty white handkerchief struck Regan as incongruous.

The woman blew her nose once, twice, three times, and then rolled her eyes. "I said to my husband, this is just our luck. We're here for, what, two days, and a fire breaks out. Brian, hold that umbrella over my head, please. My hair is getting wet."

Brian reminded Regan of a big teddy bear. He was about six foot three, with brown hair and a handsome face. He shrugged and obeyed.

"We're lucky it wasn't worse," Regan said. "No one was injured, and we should be able to get back inside pretty soon."

"Aren't you the optimist?" the woman, who sounded American, grunted. Looking at Regan as she continuously dabbed her nostrils, she asked, "What brings you here?"

"Our honeymoon," Regan answered.

"Nice," the woman answered. "We went to the Bahamas on our honeymoon three years ago. It rained all week. I mean every day. At least when you come to Ireland, you're not counting on sunshine. You're obviously American. Do you have an Irish background?"

Regan smiled. "Yes."

The woman's face lit up. "We started a business online selling memorabilia emblazoned with Irish family crests. You might want to take a look at our catalogue."

Brian pulled on his wife's arm. "Sheila, not now."

"We're standing in the rain, Brian. What else do we have to talk about? I'm certainly not keeping them from anything." She looked from Regan to Jack. "What's your last name?"

"Reilly. And mine was Reilly before I married him," Regan answered.

"Let's hope it means you're compatible."

"We are," Jack assured her.

"You know there's a ghost named Reilly who supposedly haunts this castle. A lace tablecloth she made almost two hundred years ago is upstairs in the memorabilia room. There's a little plaque about May Reilly up there. Have you seen it?"

"No. We were so tired after dinner last night, we figured we'd look in the morning."

"Who knows?—You might be related to her."

"Maybe," Regan answered.

"I'll leave you our catalogue at the front desk tomorrow. Our business is going really well. Really, really well. Let me tell you, if there's anything that people like better than the sound of their own name, it's the sight of their name on anything from plaques to dishes, to certificates explaining the family crest. And you're both Reilly. Two for the price of one! We'll even throw in a mug for free!" She laughed. "By the way, I'm Sheila O'Shea, and this is my hubby, Brian."

Introductions were made, and the men shook hands the way men do when they're not really interested in the conversation.

"Where do you live now?" Sheila asked.

"New York. And you?"

"Phoenix. I love the sunshine." She paused. "You know about our business. What do you do?" She smiled in her most friendly way, then raised her eyebrows questioningly. "Anything we can buy from you?"

"Not unless you need the services of a private investigator, which is what I am. Jack is the head of the Major Case Squad in New York City."

Sheila's smile remained plastered on her face. "Nice," she said. "Your jobs must be so interesting."

The door of the castle opened, and Neil Buckley appeared. "You can all come back inside," he announced. "Anyone whose room smells of smoke, check with Martin at the desk. We have a few vacant rooms that are far from the kitchen. And we're serving tea, coffee, and pastries in the lounge for anyone who would like an early bird breakfast."

"No, thanks," Jack whispered in Regan's ear.

The crowd surged toward the door. Most guests seemed anxious to get back to their warm beds.

"See you later," Sheila said abruptly as she and Brian hurried off.

Regan and Jack headed straight for their room. Jack unlocked the door and went into the bathroom while Regan walked directly to the window facing the lake. She paused for several minutes, staring out into the darkness.

Once they were back in bed, Jack turned to Regan. "Are you going to tell me what's on your mind? When I came out of the bathroom, you didn't even notice. You were just staring out the window."

Regan hesitated. "Jack, I know it sounds crazy."

"I'm all ears."

"Before we ran downstairs, you said it looked as if I saw a ghost. I think I did. A woman with a long dark coat and a scarf over her head was looking up at me and shaking her fist. She looked as if she belonged in another century."

Jack smiled. "You think it's May Reilly?"

"I knew you would think it's crazy, but there was something hazy about her. And then she disappeared."

"It's just so unlike you."

"I know."

A framed print slid off the wall and crashed on the floor.

They were both startled, but then Regan smiled. "Maybe I'm not so crazy after all. But I refuse to get out of bed right now."

Jack pulled her close. "So do I." He turned and called out. "Good night, May Reilly! Let us get some sleep. Tomorrow we'll admire your tablecloth."

Regan laughed. But something was making her uneasy. *Could* I really have seen a ghost? she wondered.

Down the hall, Brian and Sheila had also climbed back into bed.

"I can't believe it," Brian said. "Of all people you chose to bump into, you have to pick the investigator wife of one of the NYPD's biggest cops. What possessed you?"

"I couldn't help it! The smoke was really getting to me, and she was walking out the door right in front of us. And she was so nice. I shouldn't leave them our catalogue? Maybe they'll pass it around to their Irish friends."

"No! Of course not! With any luck they'll forget about us." Brian pulled the covers around his neck and turned off the light. "Head of the Major Case Squad," he muttered as he closed his eyes.

I should have known that this project would be too risky, he thought uneasily. We could lose everything. Especially our reputation.

But we're in too deep to back out.

I should have known.

3

There's good reason they call New York the city that never sleeps, Sergeant Keith Waters thought late Monday night as he hailed a cab outside a downtown restaurant. He would be happy to get home. It had been a hectic day at work with his boss on his honeymoon. Jack's top assistant, Keith—a handsome black man in his late thirties with boundless energy—smiled as he thought about Regan and Jack's wedding. It had been a blast. People were on the dance floor all night.

On Sunday, he'd spent the day recovering. After working until nearly 11:00 tonight, he'd gone to dinner with a couple of the guys from the office. As the taxi made its way up the West Side, he decided to check his messages at work one more time. Sometimes cases were agonizingly slow to solve. Other times they could break in an instant. Keith loved his job and, like Jack, was always checking in. It was not a nine-to-five existence.

There was one new message on his voice mail—from one of their paid informants.

"Keith, I know Jack is in Ireland on his honeymoon. I heard that those two jewel thieves, your favorite Jane and John Doe, are also aware he's in Ireland. Word is that they might be there now. They plan to ruin Jack's honeymoon by pulling something off right under his nose once again."

Keith couldn't believe it. The Does were masters of disguise, traveling all over the world and stealing jewelry wherever they went. They worked under numerous aliases. For the last seven years, since their first hit, they had eluded law enforcement. But last year their capture had become a personal crusade for Jack.

Regan and Jack had gone to a black tie reception at the Metropolitan Museum of Art. A woman lost an emerald bracelet worth $300,000. She thought it had fallen off her wrist at the cocktail party. The next day one of the museum workers found a business card tucked in the corner of a painting. It read:

WE LOVE EMERALDS. THANKS SO MUCH.
JANE AND JOHN DOE.

The thieves had obviously managed to slip the bracelet off the socialite's wrist without being detected. Regan and Jack had spoken to the seventyish woman, a well-known patron of the arts, during the cocktail hour. Regan had complimented her on the exquisite bracelet. Then when the woman sat down to dinner, she noticed the bracelet was gone. After the calling card was left, Jack realized that the thieves were probably eyeing the emeralds at the same time Regan was admiring them. A month later a valuable diamond brooch was stolen during a fund-raiser at the Chicago Art Institute, and the Doe business card was found again.

Jack was interviewed after the second theft, vowed to catch the Does, and made no bones about what he thought of their character.

They must have heard the interview, Keith thought wearily, rubbing his eyes. He hadn't planned to call Jack on his honeymoon. Heck, he knew he'd probably hear from Jack anyway. But there was no question he had to call.

Keith looked at his watch. It was 12:30, which meant it was 5:30 in the morning in Ireland. I'll set my alarm and call the boss in a few hours. He shook his head. Jane and John Doe were really out to push Jack's buttons—and on his honeymoon, no less.

He hoped they'd live to regret it.

4

At 8:30 A.M. the phone rang in Regan and Jack's room. Groggily, Jack reached over and picked it up. "Hello."

"Is this my new relation, Jack Reilly?" a man with an Irish brogue asked with great enthusiasm.

Jack rubbed his eyes with his right hand. "I'm not sure," he joked. "Who's this?"

A laugh boomed in Jack's ear. "Gerard Reilly. Regan's grandfather and my grandfather were brothers, don't you know?"

"Really."

"Indeed. Did I wake you?"

"No," Jack lied. "Not at all."

"I wanted to make sure you were all right. I just heard on the telly that there was a wee fire in Hennessy Castle last night, and I wondered if you needed to come and stay with us."

"No!" Jack answered almost too quickly. "Thank you," he added. "I think they have everything under control around here."

"Grand. Well then, I know you were planning on coming around sometime this week. Would you like to come to dinner tonight? They said it might be a day or two before the Hennessy kitchen is up and running again at full steam. My wife is making an Irish stew that is superb."

"Let me ask the boss here." Jack related the conversation to Regan and handed her the phone.

"Gerard, hello. That sounds great for tonight."

"Brilliant. How about coming at six? I think you already have the directions and such, isn't that right?"

"Yes. Thanks, Gerard. We'll see you later." Regan handed Jack the phone.

As he replaced it in the receiver, he smiled at Regan. "I'm sure your relatives are lovely people, but I don't want to spend my honeymoon with them."

"Neither do I, but tonight's a good night to have dinner with them—especially if the kitchen is out of commission."

The phone rang again.

"Maybe it's one of your cousins," Regan quipped as she pulled the blanket up under her chin. The room was gray and cold.

"Hello," Jack answered. He sat up quickly. "Keith, what's going on?"

Regan watched as a stunned expression came over Jack's face. I can only imagine what this is about, she thought.

"Let me know if you hear *anything* at all about them. You can call my cell phone at any time." He hung up.

"Jack, what is it?"

"Word is that Jane and John Doe are in Ireland and want to pull something off to embarrass me while we're here on our honeymoon."

"How do they know where we are?"

Jack shrugged. He was thinking of the large wedding announcement last Sunday in *The New York Times* and several other newspapers. But there was no mention of their honeymoon plans.

"What should we do?" Regan asked.

"Let's get dressed and go downstairs. I want to find out what happened here last night."

When Jack went in to shower, Regan got up, wrapped a robe around her, and closed the windows in the room. She picked up the picture frame that had fallen on the floor, rested it on the dressing table, and studied the sketch of the grounds of Hennessy Castle. Regan then glanced out the back window.

The lake was still, and the green lawn added some color to the dreary, gray day. All was peaceful and silent, if a little gloomy. In the distance, Regan could see one of the many islands in the large lake. A boat departed from the castle dock every morning and afternoon for an hour-long tour of Lake Hennessy.

We should do that one of these days, Regan thought.

Twenty minutes later they were both dressed. As they left the room, they encountered a young room steward in the hallway about to enter the room next door.

"Good morning," he said, nodding his head.

"Good morning," Regan answered. "There's some glass in the corner of our room. A print fell off the wall last night."

"No problem. That's the least of the hotel's problems at the moment."

"That's great," Jack muttered as he and Regan walked toward the main staircase.

Down in the lobby, the smell of smoke had diminished. The hotel was eerily quiet. It seemed that all of the other guests were still sleeping off the early morning disturbance. Regan and Jack helped themselves to coffee, which tasted wonderful. China mugs in hand, they walked through the archway to the small reception area just inside the front door, where a young woman was sitting at a computer.

"May we speak to the manager?" Jack asked.

"Certainly, sir." She stood up and disappeared through a door to a back office. The inner sanctum. The doors behind the front desks of hotels always seemed top secret, Regan thought.

Jack turned to her—"Don't worry, Regan. This honeymoon won't be all about work. I love you." As he leaned down to give her a kiss, a howl emanating from down the hall startled them both.

"Ahhhhh!" A moment later a rosy-cheeked housekeeper, wearing a gray dress and carrying a feather duster, came hurrying toward the reception desk. Her eyes were popping out of her head. "May Reilly's tablecloth is gone! Someone shattered the case in the memorabilia room and stole it! She's really going to haunt this castle now!"

Oh my God, Regan thought. I knew we should have gone up there last night.

The door to the inner sanctum flew open. A weary Neil Buckley rushed out. "For goodness' sake, Margaret Raftery, calm yourself down, woman!"

"Calm myself down!" she shrieked. "May Reilly's gorgeous tablecloth has been stolen. It's been here for almost two hundred years. There's going to be hell to pay!"

Regan and Jack followed the manager who raced up to the memorabilia room. The glass display case had been smashed. Large shards of glass covered the polished wooden floor.

Jack identified himself and Regan to a despondent Neil. "We're here to help you," he said.

"This room was locked at eleven o'clock last night," Neil explained, his voice rising. "This must have happened during all the confusion with the fire."

The housekeeper, who looked about sixty, appeared in the doorway. She was fanning herself. Sweat had broken out on her forehead.

She doesn't want to miss this, Regan thought.

"Margaret, go home if you must," Neil ordered. "The last thing I need is hysteria."

Margaret nodded and took off.

But, then again, if you can get the day off, Regan mused.

"The fire could have been started to cause a distraction," Jack suggested to Neil. "If thieves tried to steal the tablecloth during the day or even at night, someone might hear them. But with the fire alarm going off and all the confusion, they could move in quickly without being noticed."

"Have any of the hotel guests checked out this morning?" Regan asked.

"Just one elderly couple. They were so upset about the fire and too nervous to stay here." Neil's eyes widened. "As a matter of fact, they left an envelope at the desk for you, Jack."

Uh-oh, Regan thought.

They all raced back downstairs. A minute later Jack was ripping open a plain white envelope with his name on it. He pulled out a business card. Scrawled in black ink were the words

SORRY WE MISSED YOU! WE JUST LOVE LACE TABLECLOTHS, ESPECIALLY ONE MADE BY A REILLY! HAPPY HONEYMOON!

JANE AND JOHN DOE

5

"Jane and John Doe" were enjoying a gleeful morning. Driving away from Hennessy Castle in their mini Cooper as dawn broke, they had high-fived each other. Anyone who spotted them might have thought it odd to see two elderly folks engaging in a salute most often practiced by a much younger generation. But, of course, Jane and John Doe were not as old as they appeared.

They were both in their late forties.

Anna and Bobby Marston, aka Jane and John Doe, never used those names in public or on legal documents. They traveled under several aliases but had decided long ago to address each other as often as possible by the terms of endearment used by couples everywhere, monikers that wouldn't raise suspicion from anyone who heard them.

Anna was Hon.

Bobby was Sweetie.

The few people they had met in Ireland knew them as Karen and Len Cortsman.

Now, as they traveled down the old country roads, they were satisfied with a job well done. They were heading home, their home in the Emerald Isle. They had bought an isolated cottage in a small village by the sea, just south of Galway, where they would retreat after pulling off a job or two. It was easy to slip under the radar screen of law enforcement in a place where the only signs of life for miles came from the blink of a bored-looking sheep or the swinging tail of a cow munching on the endless fields of grass. The village was quite a change from the bustling streets of New York, London, and Sydney, places that Anna and Bobby usually frequented. But at the cottage they would relax, listen to their dialect tapes, and spend time on the Internet researching upcoming charity galas. To anyone who crossed their path, they appeared to be an unassuming couple who craved the simple life.

Nothing could be further from the truth.

"Sweetie," Anna said, pulling off her gray wig, "we're so daring these days."

Bobby waved his hand dismissively. "It's fun. I just wish I could see the expression on Jack Reilly's face when he reads our card. That'll teach him to refer to us as lowlifes."

"It's still pretty mean to do this on his honeymoon."

"Hon, we're mean people." Bobby started to laugh, a staccato sound that was unique and strange: *henh, henh, henh.* His cackle reminded Anna of a woodpecker. She had told him a million times to try to change his laugh, but it was useless. He was forty-one when she met him in New York City. She eventually realized there wasn't much use trying to change anything about anybody once they had hit the big four-oh.

As Bobby drove, Anna removed the gray toupee from his head and fluffed up his thick mane of brown hair. No sense looking like an elderly couple. Sooner or later, probably sooner, the police would be on the lookout for them. Anna placed the "his and hers" hairpieces in a travel bag at her feet and ran her fingers through her own stylishly cut short brown hair. She was wiry, as was Bobby, and they both were in good shape, thanks to regular workouts. She was five feet six inches tall, and he was five feet ten. There was nothing remarkable or unremarkable about their looks, which made it easy for them to both blend into crowds and change their appearance.

Anna had been a makeup artist in New York City who'd been to many wealthy people's homes to get them looking their best for anything from a television interview to a wedding or charity function. She saw how phony many of these VIPs could be. She heard them gossip about the other phonies out there. The amount of money some of them threw around was staggering.

One of her most fortuitous jobs was doing makeup for a magician who taught her a few sleight-of-hand tricks.

"You made me and my wife look good," he joked. "That's magic in itself. Let me show you a thing or two . . ."

Then she met Bobby, who had drifted from job to job over the years, occasionally making a few bucks here and there in whatever schemes he could get involved in. But those schemes had been minor until he met Anna. Halfway through dinner on their first date she held up his expensive watch and asked coyly, "Were you looking for this?"

Reflexively, he grabbed his wrist. The watch was gone! How did she do it? The woman was a genius!

He fell in love.

It wasn't long before they decided to pool their talents and go for the excitement and money that was out in the world, just waiting for them.

And in more than seven years they had never been caught.

After nearly two hours of early-morning driving on twisting, turning, two-lane country roads, they were almost at their home, a three-room dwelling that was their only permanent residence.

"What are we going to do with the lace tablecloth?" Anna asked as she dug in her purse for a piece of gum. After all those years of being two inches from people's faces, she became addicted to any form of breath mint.

Bobby shrugged. "Somebody out there will want it. It has historic value. It's nice."

"Nice? It's gorgeous. That May Reilly had talent. She was a lacemaker ahead of her time, I'll tell you that. Not too many people knew how to make lace in this country until twenty years after she died. I think I would have liked her. If she were living today, I'd love to do her makeup." Anna paused. "I bet we could find someone who would pay a lot of money for that tablecloth of hers."

"Good."

Bobby turned down the dirt path that ended at their front door.

"I get tears in my eyes whenever we return to our home by the sea," Anna said as she unwrapped the foil around her favorite spearmint gum. "It's like we're the only two people in the world when we're here. We're really living our dream. It's so peaceful. I just wish I had girlfriends to go to lunch with."

Bobby was unmoved. "This place is good for what it's good for," he said. "We spend a little down time here, and then when we're about to go nuts from the quiet, we go back out into the world again, guns blazing." He laughed his annoying laugh. "That's why I like it. The boredom motivates me."

Anna nodded. "True. What I miss most when we're here is having people to talk to.

When I was a makeup artist, people would tell me stories that would curl your toes. I enjoyed that."

"Those stories didn't pay for traveling around the world to five-star resorts," Bobby snapped as he stopped the car.

"I bet I could have sold some of them," Anna replied

"You would have if you had known me."

Inside the cottage it was damp and chilly. Anna turned on the heat, thankful they had bought a cottage with modern heating and plumbing systems. The message light on their answering machine was blinking. "Who could be calling us?" Bobby muttered as he pressed the playback button.

"Karen and Len, it's Siobhan Noonan from O'Malley's pub here. I don't know whether you're in town, but if you are, come join us this evening, if you please. Three local musicians will be performing. It'll be a good craic. You told me to let you know when we'd have live Irish music."

"There's one person we should never have talked to," Bobby scoffed.

"We had to wait so long for a table that night," Anna remembered. "It's probably a mistake for us to have more than one drink while we're sitting at the bar. Loose lips sink ships." She didn't point out that Bobby had been the one who gave Siobhan their number after gulping down his second scotch on the rocks. Siobhan's gift of the gab was dangerously infectious. "But it might be fun to go up there tonight and just relax and listen to music."

"Maybe," Bobby said, "but I'll need a nap first." He opened the back door, stepped out onto the porch, and stared out at the gray Atlantic Ocean far in the distance.

You do need a nap, Anna thought. You're getting cranky. She went and put her arms around him.

"What are you smiling about?" Bobby asked.

"I'm imagining Jack Reilly's expression if he ever found out how we knew he was coming to Ireland."

Bobby couldn't help but grin. "That would be a sight to see . . ."

6

Regan couldn't believe it. Jane and John Doe had been right here in Hennessy Castle.

"I'd like to take a look at the room where they stayed," Jack said in a controlled tone to Neil. "I hope it hasn't been cleaned yet."

"Right away!" Neil cried and barked to a clerk. "They were registered under the name Norton. What room were they in?" A moment later Neil was handed the room key. "If they stole the tablecloth, then they must have been the ones who set the fire!" he said as he motioned for Regan and Jack to follow him.

"The fire was definitely set?" Regan asked.

"Indeed! Terrible, isn't it?"

"What time did the Nortons check out?" Jack asked as they once again raced down a hallway of Hennessy Castle.

"About five A.M. Right after everyone went back to their rooms. They were so polite. It made me feel terrible that these two old folks were heading out so early on such a damp, depressing morning. I was actually worried that they'd catch a cold and tried to get them to stay. But they both insisted that they wouldn't be comfortable sleeping here after there had been a fire. . . . Those two devils are such liars!"

"They're devils all right," Jack agreed. "Did they have a car picking them up?"

"No. They said they had their own car."

"Do you have the license number?"

"Highly doubtful."

They reached the door of the room. Neil unlocked it and pushed the door open. The bed was rumpled but didn't look as if it had been slept in. The room service cart from the night before was at the foot of the bed in front of the television.

"I see they ordered the steak," Neil observed. "It's really gorgeous."

It was clear that the criminal couple had hearty appetites. The baked potato jackets had been scraped bare, traces of oil lingered on the salad plates, and only a few crumbs remained in the bread basket. Two sparkling water bottles were empty.

No drinking on the job, Regan observed.

There was no sign that the shower had been used. The sink in the bathroom had a blob of pink toothpaste stuck to its side. They came in their disguises, Regan thought, and were here to get a job done—like actors in a play. This had been the backstage area until it was showtime.

Neil, Regan, and Jack checked the room from top to bottom. There was nothing left behind. The garbage cans were empty. Jane and John Doe are pros, Regan thought.

"Neil," Jack said, "can we go back to your office and check their reservation records? I'd also like to take a look at the kitchen."

Neil nodded.

The kitchen looked like a typical large commercial kitchen. Except this one was charred. The massive stove and the wall behind it were blackened. Workers were cleaning up the mess caused by the fire and the attempts to put it out.

"Is that the cook who pulled the fire alarm?" Jack asked Neil, pointing to a guy in his mid-forties, slightly heavy, with pointed features and dark hair peeking out from under his chef's hat. He didn't look as if he was having a great day.

"Yes."

"Could we talk to him in your office?"

A second door behind the front desk led to Neil's office. It was small but cozy and, like the rest of the castle, beautifully decorated. His desk was a large wooden antique, and the chairs were leather. The plush rug had a deep red background. A small fireplace between two small windows was not lit. I guess he's in no mood for any more fires, Regan thought. But I bet he'd love to hide in here. A theft, a fire that was deliberately set, and international thieves who had been hotel guests might cause problems for Hennessy Castle's fine reputation.

Neil sat behind his desk and gestured for Regan and Jack to sit in the two chairs in front of him. He started tapping on the keys of his computer.

"They checked in at three o'clock yesterday and used the names Betty and Earl Norton. They gave their address as London."

"When did they make the reservation?" Jack asked.

"Last Friday. To stay for four nights."

"They paid with a credit card?"

"Yes."

"I'll see what my office can find out with the credit card information," Jack said. "And you don't have any information about the kind of car they were driving?"

"No, we don't require it. But I can assure you that we will in the future."

Great, Regan thought.

"I have to say I was surprised at the way the two of them were able to carry their own suitcases when they checked out. They insisted they didn't need any help. Things were so hectic around here that I didn't worry about it too much."

"They can take care of themselves," Jack said wryly.

"Did they speak with English accents?" Regan asked Neil.

"Yes. They seemed like a proper English couple."

Five minutes later a nervous Conor Devlin

came into the office. He had taken off his white apron and chef's hat.

"Conor, sit down," Neil said, pointing to the only remaining chair in the room. "We just want to talk to you for a few minutes."

"Yes, sir."

"Can you tell these folks exactly what happened this morning when you came to work? I know you've told me, but they're trying to help us out."

Conor sat and folded his hands. "I came in a little before four, like I always do to get things organized for breakfast. When I approached the kitchen, I smelled smoke. I opened the door, flipped on the light, and was shocked. Smoke was everywhere. I ran out and pulled the fire alarm, grabbed a fire extinguisher, and then ran back in. I could see the flames shooting up from the stove. I ran over, and luckily I was able to put it out." He shook his head. "Someone had poured grease into three different pans and then turned on the jets full blast."

"What do you think would have happened if you hadn't walked in there when you did?" Jack asked.

"Lord knows," Conor said. "The damage would have been much worse, I suppose."

"I wonder if whoever did this could have known that you come in at four every day."

"I don't have any idea," Conor answered. "Seems strange, doesn't it?" he asked, not expecting an answer.

Jack turned to Neil. "Is the kitchen locked at night?"

"'Tis. But someone had fiddled with the lock."

Jack sighed. "I'd like to talk to any of your staff who had contact with the Nortons. Someone must have brought them to their room. Someone must have delivered room service. We've got to find out if there is anything anyone remembers about them that might help. If they were willing to set a fire that could have easily gotten out of control, I can only imagine what else they might have planned."

7

Sheila and Brian were also roused from their sleep by the ringing of a telephone, Brian's international cell phone. But their call wasn't from a friendly cousin or coworker. It was from someone they had made a business deal with, a deal that was already making them queasy.

Dermot Finnegan was on the line from Phoenix, Arizona. A sixty-five-year-old multi-millionaire, Finnegan was a formidable character known for his charm as well as his temper. He'd emigrated from Ireland with his parents when he was twelve. Scrappy and tenacious, he had worked hard to earn money for his family from the day he set foot on American soil. And he had never stopped. Retirement held no interest for him. From his thirty-room mansion on a golf course, he was still wheeling and dealing, occasionally heading out for a round of golf, which he almost always won.

He could be a bit of a tyrant when things didn't go his way.

"Brian," Dermot yelled into the phone. "It sounds like you're still asleep! By my calculation it's past nine o'clock there. What are you still doing in bed?"

Brian sat up. "There was a fire in the hotel in the middle of the night."

"A fire?"

"Yes. A grease fire in the kitchen."

"You're not going to let a little fire stop you from completing your mission, are you?"

"Of course not," Brian answered, rolling his eyes. Dermot was also known for talking to his employees about their "mission," whether it was cleaning his house or carrying out his deals. Brian could just picture Dermot with a cigar hanging out of his mouth, his piercing blue eyes wide open, his face flushed. Dermot had a full head of dyed brown hair and a body that would benefit from walking around the golf course once in a while instead of always being chauffeured in a cart with a Rolls-Royce grill and heavily padded seats.

"When are you picking up the paintings?"

"This afternoon," Brian told him for the hundredth time.

"And you're flying back immediately?"

"Yes."

"You're sure you can't get the artist to come with you?"

"I told you she's a nun who lives in a convent that is practically cloistered."

"Practically cloistered—you're either cloistered or you're not," Dermot growled.

"Listen, she doesn't want her identity to be revealed. It's a miracle we got her to paint these seven paintings as it is."

"I don't know why. Look at the Book of Kells, those beautiful illuminated manuscripts on display for everyone to see at Trinity College in Dublin. It's no secret that was done by monks. What's this nun's problem?"

"She made us promise."

"Promises are made to be broken. We'll work on that later. This is just phase one of our project. I'm telling you, she paints like an angel. It was very generous of you to donate her painting for the auction at my Irish Eyes fund-raiser." He laughed. "I bet you didn't know what valuable art you had."

He was right, but Brian wouldn't admit it. "You know Sheila and I like to support Irish causes. We paid a lot of money for that painting," he lied.

"You *should* be generous to the Irish, making money off all that junk you have the nerve to call Irish memorabilia."

"Listen, Dermot, I promise to call you as soon as we have the paintings. Okay?"

"All right. Now talk to that nun. See if she'll give at least one interview. And tell her I'll build her a convent here in Phoenix where she can paint all day. The weather's much better here than it is in Ireland."

"She's not interested."

"I can't understand it! There's a lot of money to be made off her talent, as you know. I noticed you wasted no time in cashing the check I gave you when I ordered the paintings."

"Did you expect me to put the money in a drawer?"

"Of course not. But it was a broad leap of faith on my part to write you that check. A half million dollars is a lot of money. I want those paintings in my house here in sunny Arizona as soon as possible. It's not often that an exciting new talent is discovered. I should take over Sotheby's." He hung up.

Brian closed the cell phone, dropped it next to him on the bed, and rubbed his eyes. "I didn't know getting involved with Dermot would be such a headache."

"I only wish I'd taken an art appreciation course along the way," Sheila said wistfully. "If we had known how valuable that painting was, we never would have given it away, and we could have exploited 'Sister' on our own." She laughed. "I can't believe you told him the artist is a nun."

"What else was I going to say? If Dermot met the real artist, the mystique would be gone."

"True. But that Dermot is sharp. He knows the value of things. I can't tell a tacky key chain from the seventh wonder of the world. But when I find something I can put a family name on, I go for it!" She reached over and picked up the phone beside the bed. "I'll order a pot of coffee to have while we're getting showered and dressed." She pressed a button and waited. "Hello, I'd like to order room service—"

The clerk cut her off. "Sorry, no room service this morning."

"What?" Sheila whined.

"No room service. A limited breakfast is being served in the dining room. Terribly sorry."

Sheila sighed and hung up the phone. "No room service. That's just great." She shook her head. "I've always enjoyed our stays at Hennessy Castle, but this time I can't wait to get out of here."

"For a lot of reasons," Brian agreed. "Let's hope we don't run into the Reillys this morning."

Sheila did not give him the satisfaction of an answer.

Brian forcefully threw back the covers. "I won't be able to breathe easily until we hand over those paintings to old man Finnegan."

"I can't wait to finally see them," Sheila said excitedly, then laughed. "Over at the convent . . ."

8

A young bellman named Liam, who had been the one to bring Jane and John Doe's bags to their room when they had checked in, was ushered into Neil's office. In his early twenties, tall and lanky, with a round face, twinkling eyes, and a quick smile, Liam clearly enjoyed the excitement of being questioned about the two suspected criminals.

"They had a big black suitcase on wheels and two tote bags," he began. "I loaded them onto the cart, and as we walked to their room, I told them about all the amenities Hennessy Castle has to offer, as I always do."

Neil nodded approvingly.

"You know, people like to hear about the spa and room service, that kind of thing. Then I asked them where they were coming in from. They said London."

"Did they have English accents?" Regan asked.

"Yes. They sounded like the queen!—like they had plums in their mouths. They walked very slowly, and the lady said she was tired from the flight and wanted to take a nap and order room service for dinner. When we got to their room, I offered to get them ice, but they weren't interested. He gave me a good tip. That was it."

"Was there anything unusual about them?" Jack asked. "Anything they said or did that you remember?"

Liam's baby face looked thoughtful. "Let's see. . . . Oh, there was one thing that kind of struck me," he said with enthusiasm as he recalled the memory. "When I took their suitcase and hoisted it onto the luggage rack in their room, I noticed that it didn't have any tags on it. Like it hadn't been checked in at the airport. Some people rip the tags off right away when they unpack; others leave them on until their next trip. But they said they had just come from the airport. Believe me, I see all kinds of suitcases. Some are pretty nice, and others are pretty ratty. Have you ever seen a suitcase that's taped up because the zipper's broken?" Liam laughed heartily. "It always surprises me. You think that people who could afford to stay at Hennessy Castle would spring for luggage that doesn't look as if it's been run over by an eighteen-wheeler."

"We don't have many of those," Neil said, his tone flat and disapproving.

"No, we don't, we don't," Liam agreed quickly. "Not a-tall. Indeed. No way. The guests here are lovely."

"Did the other bags have tags or anything you noticed about them?" Jack interrupted.

The bellman closed his eyes and nodded, trying not to laugh again. "Oh, dear, this is going to sound mean."

"What?" Jack asked. "Just say it."

"I live down in Galway. They had a road race recently, a mini-marathon, if you will. My girlfriend and I ran in it. It was freezing cold. When you crossed the finish line, they gave out funny little decals to stick on your gym bag. It's a cartoon of runners piling up as they cross the finish line. One of those decals was on one of their tote bags. I couldn't believe it."

"Are you sure it was the decal from the race?"

"Yes! Can you imagine? The woman did nothing but complain about her aches and pains as they slowly shuffled down the hall. I thought I'd never get back to the front desk. I never dreamt her aches and pains could come from jogging! I just can't picture them in a 5K. It takes all kinds, doesn't it?"

"When was the race?" Jack asked.

"Hmmm, last November."

"November?"

"Yes."

"You didn't comment to them about the decal?"

"No. I thought it would be rude. I didn't think they could make it to the bed, never mind run a race. Also, I noticed the decal right before I left the room. They seemed like they wanted to be left alone."

At least it's a start, Regan thought. No luggage tags and a decal that put them in Galway last November. "Do you think you could get us one of those decals?" she asked.

"Sure. I have one and so does my girl-friend. It really is the way everyone looks at the end of one of those races. Miserable.

You'd never guess that running is supposed to release those happy hormones."

Jack thanked Liam for his help and exchanged numbers with him.

"I'll bring the decal to work with me tomorrow," Liam offered as he stood and shook their hands. "If you need it before, just give me a ring."

"Great," Jack said. "By the way, do you have to register to run in that race?"

"You're supposed to, but a lot of people decide to run at the last minute and jump in."

"Thanks again, Liam."

Neil nodded. "Back to the job, Liam."

"Yes, sir." When he opened the door to leave, Conor, the chef, was about to tap on it. Liam walked past him.

"Sorry to bother you," Conor said, "but I was just on the blower with the supplier from Dublin. They can't get a new stove to us before the end of the week at the earliest."

"The end of the week!" Neil cried. "An hour ago they said it wouldn't be a problem to get one out here by tomorrow!"

"They made a mistake. Turns out the one they had in stock is broken. They don't have many stoves that size just sitting around." Conor nodded in the direction of the reception area. "Word is spreading that our menu is going to be quite limited. People are getting upset."

"Who told the guests?" Neil asked as he jumped out of his chair.

"You know how it is around here . . ." Conor mumbled as Regan and Jack followed Neil out of his office.

In the lobby, a new bout of hysteria was breaking out. "We're outta here," one man cried, full of spit and vinegar. "I came here for the great food. My wife can barely boil water. This was supposed to be a treat. We'll find a hotel that can at least serve us a meal!"

"We're leaving, too!" another couple cried. "We'd be better off camping."

"We'll do our best," Neil began. "There's a pub down the road that serves a lovely shepherd's pie. We have arranged for our guests to have dinner there tonight, if you like, and hopefully we'll get a new stove by tomorrow." But he knew it was no use. Until they had a working kitchen, no one would want to stay at the castle. The guests crowding around the front desk were becoming increasingly mutinous, and it would probably be better if they just packed up and left.

Neil turned to Regan and Jack. "Will you be leaving?"

"No," Jack said firmly. "We're going to track down Jane and John Doe, but we're not going to desert you, Neil. It's because of me that you're in this mess."

"You're right about that," Neil said wearily.

Regan was glad that Jack wanted to stay. Besides the hunt for Jane and John Doe, she was determined to find out more about May Reilly—and whoever it was she had seen on the back lawn last night.

9

When Margaret Raftery left Hennessy Castle, she jumped on her bike and pedaled as fast as she could to the graveyard at the edge of the village. She went directly to May Reilly's tombstone and crossed herself.

"May," she began, her Irish brogue thick. "I'm so sorry about your tablecloth. So very, very sorry. I heard how hard you worked on it. And you never got paid! I don't blame you for haunting the castle. You should. It's only right." The words were tumbling out of her mouth.

A gusty wind caused Margaret to wrap her dark wool coat tighter around her generous frame. The graveyard was eerily quiet; the tombstones, like the weather, were damp and dark. The ground was covered with slate. The little graveyard had reached maximum capacity over a hundred years ago. No tearful relatives were left on this earth to come and pay their respects. They had all been called home as well, wherever that home turned out to be. Now it was tourists armed with cameras who walked among these tombstones, snapping photos of the age-old grave markers.

There was another graveyard a mile north on the other side of the village; it was where Margaret's parents were buried.

Margaret had heard endless stories from her mother over the years, stories dating back to May's time, about the villagers who had spent their lives in this little town called Surry and were laid to rest in the village's small graveyard. A deeply superstitious woman, Bridie would sit by the fire, knitting yet another scratchy scarf, as she recounted the tales of the local folks again and again.

"The Sullivan boy was a wonderful fellow. You've seen his grave, dear. The girl he fell head over heels for was so beautiful. What a love match. But he died from a flu bug he caught on his honeymoon. His mother said that when she heard the wailing of the banshee before his death, she was sure that it was her husband who was about to go. She went crazy with grief. The high-pitched cry of the banshee could drive anyone insane because, after all, they're only heard when a family member is about to die. . . .

"That one was a fright to work for. They never found his body. They think he was taken away by the fairies who . . .

"He spent every night in the pub, glued to a stool. His wife was such a pill. I have to say I don't blame him for never wanting to go home. But when he started gambling, that was the end."

But Bridie's favorite topic was the legend of May Reilly. "Now there was a woman. Raised by an uncle who took her in after her parents died. Learned lace making from a nun who'd come from France. And this was years before lace making became so popular. It's a shame it was so late in life when she finally put her lace-making talent to use. If May Reilly had lived longer, who knows what she could have accomplished. What they did to her . . . disgraceful! You'll never find another lace tablecloth like hers. Never!

And she's never going to rest in peace. One way or another, that Hennessy family was responsible for her passing. They worked her to death!"

When Margaret went to work at Hennessy Castle forty years ago, her mother had been wary. Margaret still remembered her mother's words: "Did you forget that May Reilly was a housekeeper for the Hennessys? Look what happened to her! Be careful, Margaret. There are ill winds blowing around those grounds. There is evil within those walls. The Hennessy family never had any luck after May died. I'm telling you, that place is cursed!"

"But, Mother, it's a job," Margaret had argued.

"'Tis. But just know what you're getting yourself into."

"May Reilly's trouble came after she made the Hennessys a tablecloth. They didn't think she deserved extra money because they were already paying her as their housekeeper."

Her mother had looked Margaret in the eye and warned, "It may not be today or tomorrow, but something will happen. Mark my words."

Alone in the graveyard, Margaret cried out, "Mother was right! She was always right! May Reilly, I will do right by you! Do the right thing!" she said, pronouncing it as *ting.*

Margaret hopped back on her bike and pedaled through the main street of the village to the tiny road that led out of town. In the distance a rolling field of green stretched out as far as the eye could see. Her little cottage was three miles away. Margaret pedaled hard, willing herself to go faster and faster. When she passed her parents' graveyard, guilt washed over her. Sadly, it wasn't an unfamiliar feeling. She turned her bike around, steered it across the grass to her parents' grave, and said a quick prayer. She said an even shorter one for her late husband, whose grave was three stones down. Angus hadn't been the world's best mate. For thirty-eight years Margaret had cooked and cleaned for him, raised their son who now lived in Dublin, all the while working as a housekeeper at the castle. But Angus kept his feelings inside except when it came to discouraging her about what she loved to do. "It's as useful as a lighthouse on a bog," he'd always tell her. Maybe he was right after all!

"I should have left May and the vision of her tablecloth alone," Margaret said aloud.

She rode bumpily out of the graveyard, doing her best to avoid getting stuck in the mud. I've got to get home, she thought frantically. I've got to get home and do right by May!

One thought comforted her.

Whoever stole that tablecloth had no idea what they were in for.

10

The madding crowd around the front desk was growing.

"Regan, before we do anything else, let's see what they're offering for breakfast," Jack suggested.

"Sounds good to me."

They circumvented the disgruntled guests and headed for the dining room. After they were seated, Regan looked up and saw Sheila and Brian, the couple they'd met in the middle of the night, appear in the doorway. When they spotted Regan and Jack, they quickly waved, then turned and left the dining room.

"That was odd," Regan noted.

"They probably went to get their cata-logue," Jack said sardonically. "Let's eat fast."

"Jack!" Regan couldn't help but laugh.

By the time they finished a breakfast of Irish soda bread, fruit, coffee, and juice, Sheila and Brian hadn't reappeared. The Reillys headed to their room, and Jack immediately called his office.

"I can't believe it, boss!" Keith said after hearing about the Does. "They struck fast. I should have called you right away, but I didn't want to wake you. It would have been about five-thirty in the morning."

"Don't worry about it," Jack told him. "They were gone by then." He gave Keith the credit card number and the alias the Does had used at the castle. "You can add that to the list of the aliases they've used around the world. Check out the credit card information. Let our contacts know they were in Ireland as of a few hours ago. I hope we can come up with something concrete to help us locate them. The only lead we have is the decal that indicates they spent time in Galway."

"I'll get right on it. Hey, don't let this ruin your honeymoon."

"I'm with Regan," Jack said, reaching over

and giving her hand a squeeze. "We'll manage to make the most of it." After he hung up, he turned to her. "So, Mrs. Reilly. We know they had the decal from the road race in Galway. Any suggestions?"

"Let's drive down to Galway and take a look around. Gerard will be thrilled if we tell him we'll be there early. He's the eyes and ears of Galway. Maybe we can find out more about that race."

Jack put his hand on Regan's cheek. "To think we made a pact to put this kind of craziness behind us on our honeymoon."

Regan smiled. "We were planning to explore Ireland. Now we *really* get to explore it."

"As we search for an average-looking middle-aged couple who constantly change their look, use different accents, and steal jewelry whenever they get the chance. Should be fun."

Regan frowned. "I can't believe they've gotten away with this for so long," she said. "We came to Ireland to look for our roots, and instead we're searching for a couple who don't seem to have any. As they say, a rolling stone gathers no moss."

"But can they sit still for a while?" Jack asked thoughtfully. "Ireland is becoming more modern all the time, but it's still a place where you can disappear. In this area it's as if time stood still. Ireland would be a good place to hide. They may be spending time somewhere around Galway, but how could they have known that we were going to be here?"

They both sat in silence.

Galway, Regan thought. Galway. Slowly a horrible thought entered her consciousness. She blanched and pushed the preposterous idea out of her head.

"Let's get going," Jack said. "We'll enlist that cousin of yours to help us find the Does—before they take off on us again." He stood and pulled Regan up.

She walked over to the dressing table by the window to pick up her purse. The image of the ghostly figure on the back lawn kept running through her head. She had appeared just around the time the tablecloth was stolen. Regan wanted to talk to the housekeeper about the legend of May Reilly, but that would have to wait. Regan smiled to herself. Catching John and Jane Doe wasn't about the tablecloth, but she was somehow sure that May Reilly would be happy if they brought it back in one piece.

11

As soon as Sheila and Brian spotted the Reillys in the dining room, they went back to their room, grabbed their coats, and hurried down to the car.

"Let's get a real Irish breakfast," Brian said, disgust in his tone.

"Who wants cold cereal anyway?" Sheila said in agreement. "Maybe one of the village pubs will be open." She pulled down the sun visor, checked her lipstick in the mirror, and fluffed her bangs. "Once we pick up the paintings this afternoon, we'll be home free. Back to Arizona. Back to our normal life." She flipped the visor back up.

"Normal life," Brian grunted.

"Don't you think it's normal? We've been married three years, and already we have a nice house where it's warm, I have my memorabilia business going, and you have a good job selling stocks. We're respected members of the community."

"We're not going to be respected if this doesn't work out," Brian said. "Getting involved with Dermot was not a good idea. Spending his money on a warehouse full of Irish tchotchkes was not a good idea. Ripping off this artist was not a good idea."

"We needed the money to get my business off the ground," Sheila said. "She'll never know the difference."

Brian didn't agree, but he said nothing. They drove into the village in silence and discovered that the two pubs didn't open until 11:30. There was no sign of life out on the street.

"Someplace must serve breakfast. Let's ask at the pharmacy," Sheila suggested.

The bell on the door tinkled as they walked into the tiny, narrow store. A female pharmacist with cropped brown hair, dressed in jeans, a sweater, and a white jacket, greeted them from behind a small counter. "May I help you?" she asked in a no-nonsense manner that reminded Sheila of her pharmacist back home. Do pharmacists think everyone who walks in is a potential drug dealer? Sheila wondered.

"We're staying at Hennessy Castle, and they had a fire in the kitchen last night—" Sheila began.

"So I heard. What a shame. It could have been a lot worse. Are you feeling anxious? I have an herbal mix you can put in some tea. It'll have you feeling better in no time."

Sheila smiled. "Actually, we're okay with the experience, but right now we'd love to get a nice hot breakfast. Do you know of a place around here where we could go?"

The pharmacist eyed them quickly. "As a matter of fact, I do. Go down to the corner," she pointed, "and take a left. Four miles down the road there's a farmhouse where they serve breakfast. It's very casual." She wrote down the exact address.

"Thank you so much," Sheila said, grabbing a bottle of hand lotion from a shelf. "I'll take this." She laughed, not exactly sure why she was laughing.

"It's wonderful, that lotion." The pharmacist pressed the keys on an ancient cash register. "Makes your skin feel smooth as silk."

In the car, Brian asked, "Don't you have enough lotion in the bathroom back at the hotel?"

"Thanks to her we'll get a hot breakfast this morning," Sheila said. "Since we weren't going to buy her herbs, I thought we should at least buy something I'd eventually use."

Brian shrugged.

After a ten-minute drive down the winding country road, they located the farmhouse. Clucking chickens greeted their car as they pulled into the yard. There wasn't a human being in sight nor a sign that breakfast was being served, never mind a sign boasting how many million breakfasts they had served. A horse wandered over to the fence nearby and stared at them. The farmhouse looked slightly rundown.

"She said it was casual," Sheila muttered as they got out of the car and headed to the door. It was opened by a slightly hunched heavyset woman who was wiping her hands on her apron. She was wearing a blue cardigan sweater and a long dark skirt. Her straight gray hair was parted on the side and fell to her shoulders. She crinkled her ice blue eyes. "You're here for breakfast, are you?"

It wasn't a question, but Sheila answered in the affirmative.

"Come on in," she said, turning away.

She doesn't seem rude, but it's not exactly service with a smile, Sheila thought as they stepped into the farmhouse kitchen. It was clearly not the kitchen of a bustling restaurant. Framed embroidered proverbs about life and love and friendship covered the walls, along with family photos and religious pictures. The counters were filled with cookie jars, knickknacks, newspaper clippings, and what Sheila believed was a toaster hidden under a protective crocheted covering. A wooden hutch was crammed with teacups, saucers, and dishes and plates of various sizes and patterns. A fire was burning in a large stone fireplace at the opposite end of the room. The effect was one of cozy clutter.

"Make yourself at home," the woman said, pointing to a long wooden table with dozens of names carved into it. A bench flanked the table on either side. "My name is Philomena Gallagher. You like eggs and Irish sausage?"

"Sounds great," Brian answered quickly, doing his best to sound enthused. He and Sheila exchanged a glance. They were in a complete stranger's kitchen, and she was about to cook them breakfast. No ancient cash register was in sight. How would anyone know to come here for a meal? It was too weird, even for a small village. They were both tempted to bolt. This woman could pull a gun out of the drawer and shoot us both, Brian thought.

But they were starving. Their appetites were stronger than their fears.

They sat down, and in short order the woman served them fried eggs, tangy Irish sausage, warm scones with homemade jam, and freshly brewed coffee. "God bless you," she said when she put the food on the table, then walked back to the sink.

They ate in silence. The only sound was the loud ticking of a cuckoo clock in the hallway. Brian winked at Sheila. The food was wonderful and lifted their spirits.

Carrying a cup of tea, the woman walked over to the table and with a loud sigh sat down with them. "You folks touring around?" she asked, smiling for the first time. It was as though she had completed her job—cooking their breakfast—and now that she was done, she could talk. A multitasker she was not.

"Yes," Sheila answered, patting her lips with a cloth napkin. "This breakfast is wonderful," she said. "Have you been in the business for long?"

"What business?"

"The restaurant business."

The woman shook her head. "I'm not in the restaurant business."

Brian and Sheila both looked perplexed.

"But why—" Brian began.

The woman waved her weathered hand at them. "It's my pleasure to feed you. My grandson is staying with me for the week. He's doing a project for school, a study of people who come to visit Ireland, but we don't run into that many out on the farm here."

I'll say, Brian thought.

"My friend at the pharmacy just loves Kieran. He helps her out sometimes at the store. So she sends people my way. She knows I'm a good cook." Philomena laughed. "But yesterday I served afternoon tea to a couple who'd gone horseback riding and then into the pharmacy for Ben-Gay. They didn't think these benches were so comfortable. Too bad about them. They didn't like answering questions, either. Now you two wouldn't mind if my grandson took your picture and asked a few questions, would you?" She didn't wait for an answer but got up and moved slowly toward the hall-way. "Kieran!" she called, disappearing down the hall. "Kie-rannnnnnnn."

Sheila and Brian looked at each other with alarm. "Don't give too much information," Brian said, his tone grim. "It's just not a good idea when we're—"

A skinny red-haired kid who looked about ten came barreling into the kitchen with his video camera. "Hey, hey, hey, hey, Holly-wood," he cried as he started taping them. He reminded Sheila of the bratty next-door neighbor she had known growing up outside Boston, who'd thankfully moved away before they were teenagers. Twenty years later she married him.

'Kieran, calm down now," his grandmother ordered as she came back into the kitchen. "Can I get you more coffee?" she asked her visitors.

"No, we're fine," Sheila said.

"Get started with your questions, Kieran. They'll want to be on their way soon."

"Okay, Granny." He sat on the bench directly across from Brian and Sheila, and turned his camera on them.

This is what reality TV has done to the world, Brian thought. You're not safe from cameras anywhere.

"What are your names?" Kieran asked, sounding like a police interrogator.

This kid is a nudge, Sheila thought, but she answered politely: "We're Sheila and Brian."

"Last names?"

"Funny you should ask. Both of us actually have an Irish background in common, and that's why we love to visit Ireland."

The kid didn't blink. He obviously had his set of questions and didn't listen to the answers. He wasn't unlike most adults. "What do you plan to take advantage of when you're here?"

A local artist, Brian thought as he cleared his throat and started to answer. "What everyone does . . . the beautiful scenery, the wonderful people, shopping for Waterford crystal, hiking, the Aran Islands, and of course Dublin. Your grandmother's cooking was the biggest treat so far."

"My granny is a better cook than my mom," he said.

Philomena Gallagher smiled.

His mother must be her daughter-in-law, Sheila thought. "Where do you live, Kieran?" she asked, anxious to turn the conversation to his life.

"In a village down by Cork," he answered. "Where do you live?"

"In the summertime we like to go to Cape Cod."

"I didn't ask you that."

"Kieran, don't be rude."

"I'm not, Granny. My teacher said to find out where people come from. She didn't answer the question!"

"We grew up near Boston," Sheila answered. "It snows a lot there. Did you know that?"

"No."

"Well, it does. I met Brian when we were about your age." Sheila laughed. "He used to pelt me with snowballs on the way home from school."

"Do you have children?"

"Not yet."

"What are you waiting for?"

"Kieran!"

"Sorry, Granny."

"We've been married only a few years. I'm

sure we'll have a baby before too much longer. Kieran is such a nice name," Sheila said sweetly. "If we have a boy, maybe we'll name him Kieran."

Kieran, like most ten-year-old boys in a similar situation, couldn't have cared less. "You had relatives in Ireland who moved to America?"

"Yes. A long time ago. One of my great-grandfathers sailed to New York in 1884." She turned to Brian. "Didn't one of your great-grandfathers leave Ireland around the same time?"

"I don't know," Brian answered testily.

Sheila made a face at him and then said to Kieran, "We're both very proud of our Irish backgrounds. Now we only have time for a few more questions." God, she thought, I sound like I'm holding a press conference.

"Let me think of some good ones," Kieran said.

Philomena jumped at the chance to speak. You'd never have known it was the same woman who had said hardly two words when they walked in. "I have a son who moved to America," she said proudly. "He's doing so well, he is. He lives in New York and just loves it. I miss him, but he comes home a couple of times a year." She pointed to a picture on the wall of a young man with a woman and two small children. "He has a big job. Thankfully, it's not like the olden days when the young folks left for America. Families often never saw them again. They used to hold what were called 'American wakes' for them before they left Ireland. Did you know that?"

"How sad," Sheila said. "That is really sad. We moved out to Phoenix, and I miss seeing my mother more often."

Brian kicked her under the table.

"Stop the lights!" Kieran exclaimed, seizing on the information. "So you live in Phoenix!"

This kid is a regular Columbo, Brian thought.

"Kieran," his grandmother said, "now what are your final questions?"

"Are you rich?"

"Kieran, that's enough!"

"Okay. Sorry."

Brian stood. "I hate to cut this short, but we have an appointment to join a tour group to Galway and we're going to be late. I don't want to miss a minute of it."

Sheila stood as well. "This was so much

fun. What do we owe you for breakfast? It was delicious."

"Nothing. It was our pleasure," Philomena insisted. "Fiona down at the pharmacy told me you're staying at Hennessy Castle. Is that right?"

"Yes," Sheila gulped.

'It's grand, isn't it?'

"Yes." Sheila turned toward the door and stopped dead in her tracks. A small painting that must have been painted by *their* artist was hanging on the wall. She hadn't noticed it on the way in, and it was to her back as she ate. Philomena's painting was similar to the one they had put up for auction—a lush Irish landscape with a table set for dinner out in a field. The table was covered with an intricate lace tablecloth. The artist's initials were in the corner—their artist's initials.

The woman noticed Sheila's gaze. "Lovely, isn't it? A friend of mine gave it to me. She incorporates lace in all her paintings. Some of them are really quirky and fun. She just gives them away to her friends. I tease her that she could be the next Grandma Moses, but she's too shy.."

Sheila nodded. "It's beautiful. We've really got to be on our way." She reached out her hand. "Mrs. Gallagher, I can't tell you how much we appreciate the wonderful breakfast. Your Irish hospitality is to be admired. I hope someday we can return the favor."

"Maybe you can. If Kieran has any more questions for you, he can ring you up at the castle. I know he'd love to go by there and have a look."

"I've never been inside," Kieran cried. "I want to see the ghost!"

"That's enough," his grandmother said sternly.

"I do. I want to interview the ghost!"

"Just give us a call," Sheila replied quickly as she and Brian hurried out the door and raced to their car. She dropped into the passenger seat and tried to catch her breath. "I can't believe one of those valuable paintings is just squashed into the corner like that. It's practically hidden between the refrigerator and the door. And that kid!"

Brian threw the car into reverse and backed down the long driveway, dirt flying in all directions. "I always told you there's no such thing as a free lunch—in this case, breakfast. At least the kid didn't get our last name. We have to get those paintings and get out of here fast. Dermot's not the only one who realizes the artist's potential. I wonder who else has her paintings hanging on their walls around here." He tore down the road. "Let's drive by our girl's house right now, just to make sure we know where it is. She won't be home until four, but I'm getting anxious. You have the directions, right?"

Sheila dug them out of her purse.

Ten minutes later they found the cottage, which stood alone off the winding country road. A cluster of trees surrounded it. "There's smoke coming out of the chimney," Sheila said. "I thought that—"

"Let's ring the bell and see if she came home early," Brian interrupted. A minute later they were knocking at the door.

A wild-eyed Margaret Raftery answered, huffing and puffing. She still had on the gray dress and white apron that was her uniform at Hennessy Castle.

"Hello, Margaret. We saw the smoke in the chimney and thought you might be home," Sheila explained. "We're here to pick up our paintings."

"Forget your paintings! I just finished ripping them to pieces! They're burning in my fireplace at this very moment!"

"What?" Brian thundered. "We paid you!"

"You can have your seven hundred euros back. I have it all here for you!" She turned and ran from the door.

They quickly followed Margaret inside her tiny cottage. Brian raced over to the fireplace where giant flames were hungrily licking the shredded paintings. Before his eyes the canvases curled up and turned to ash. "Why did you do this?" he cried. "*Why*?"

"I don't want to be cursed by May Reilly. I should never have copied her special lace pattern in my paintings! It was wrong, I tell ya. It was wrong! And to take money for the paintings was a sin! You should never have asked me to." She pulled crumpled bills out of a piggy bank and threw them in the air. "Get out of here!" Margaret spotted the mug with the Raftery crest that Sheila and Brian had recently sent her. She ran over, grabbed the mug from the shelf, and flung it into the fire like a woman possessed.

"I resent that!" Sheila said. "We gave that to you out of the kindness of our hearts."

"Hmph," Margaret protested. "When I met you last November at Hennessy Castle, I thought you were such a lovely couple. I told you I'd designed the decal for the Fun Run that you had on your dresser. You made me feel so good when you said you loved it. So I gave you one of my paintings. Now you've ruined my life."

Brian's face was turning beet red. Sheila was afraid he might have a heart attack.

"We want your paintings," he said to Margaret, his voice shaking. "We don't want our money back. We made a deal with you. A deal's a deal."

"I don't care about your deal!"

The sight of her fast-talking young American stockbroker husband from Arizona trying to discuss deals with a superstitious older woman from rural Ireland was making Sheila light-headed. This was a nightmare. They'd never be able to pay back Dermot anytime soon, and he'd find out they had lied to him. He would definitely ruin their lives. She did the only thing she could think of to get this woman's sympathy.

She fell to the floor in a faint.

12

Down in their cottage by the sea, Hon and Sweetie both took long hot showers, washing their hair that had been matted down by the wigs and getting rid of all the traces of their old-age makeup. Wrapped in white terry cloth robes, they lay down on their four-poster bed, exhausted. Neither one of them had slept all night, and now, as the high of pulling off another job was starting to wear off, they were both ready to crash.

"Even though these jobs are fun, they're stressful," Bobby said quietly. "I'd love it if we could go to a health club this afternoon and work out, but it's not a good idea to be seen too much in public places."

Anna shrugged. "Yeah. But it's nice that at least we can run on the beach and along the cliffs, and enjoy the Irish seaside while we're here. Think of all those great health clubs at the hotels we've stayed in all over the world. We'll be working out at another one of those clubs soon."

"We have to figure out where to go next," Bobby said as they both drifted off. When they woke a few hours later, they were still tired but knew they wouldn't be able to sleep again until the evening. They were in that half-awake, half-asleep zone that makes people miserable.

"You want me to make blueberry pancakes?" Anna asked groggily.

"Why not?"

"Don't get too enthused," she said.

"I'd be delighted to have your delicious blueberry pancakes. The thought of them makes my mouth water."

"That's better."

The cottage was small but charming, having been refurbished before they bought it. The kitchen, dining area, and lounge were all part of the main room, with a large hearth fireplace at one end. Bobby turned on the television while Anna went to the kitchen. She put on the kettle, poured pancake mix into a bowl, and was reaching in the refrigerator for the milk and eggs when Bobby called out to her.

"Come here!"

Anna hurried over. A picture of Hennessy Castle was on the screen. The anchor was reporting on the theft of the valuable historic tablecloth and the fire that had been deliberately set. "We'll continue to follow the story," the anchor assured the audience. He turned to his coanchor. "Hopefully those thieves will be caught and—"

Bobby pressed the mute button.

"Where's the suitcase with the tablecloth?" Anna asked, her hand on her hip.

"It's still in the car."

"We should bring it inside."

Bobby grimaced. He was stretched out on the couch. He knew she meant that he should be the one to get it. "I'll go outside later. Who's going to steal a suitcase from our car? We're in the middle of nowhere."

"Somebody like us," Anna said. "We're willing to steal anytime, anywhere."

Grunting, Bobby got up from the couch. He opened the front door and went out to the car in his bare feet. He rushed back in a moment later. "It's gone!"

"What?" Anna cried.

"Just kidding." He turned and went back outside.

"You're such a riot," Anna muttered, her heart beating fast. She and Bobby had recently watched one of those shows about life in a woman's prison. It wasn't a pretty picture. Sleeping on a bunk bed? Wearing an orange jumpsuit? What was really sobering was that one woman was in for eight months for stealing $15,000 worth of jewelry. With all the jewelry she and Bobby had stolen, they'd be locked up for a hundred lifetimes. If anyone connected them to the theft of the Hennessy Castle tablecloth, the jig would be up.

Maybe trying to embarrass Jack Reilly wasn't such a great idea after all. They certainly didn't get any valuable jewelry out of it.

Bobby came back in, unzipped the suitcase, and removed the tablecloth. "This is a beauty," he said, starting to unfold it. He whistled. "It would make a great Mother's Day present. It's way too big for Mom's dinette table, but she'd figure something out." He laughed. "She can bring it to the bingo hall. The table there could handle this baby. B-12," he called out. "O-75 . . ."

"She's not going to get the tablecloth," Anna snapped. "We're not removing it from here ever."

Bobby looked up at her. "What's with you? You said before that we should sell it. I'm just kidding about my mother. We haven't even seen her in more than a year." He laughed his annoying laugh. "I think she secretly suspects we work for the CIA."

Anna stirred the pancake mix. "What else is she going to think with our lifestyle? My mother thinks I married an international consultant. I retired from doing makeup to travel the world with my man."

"You did." Bobby gently placed the tablecloth on the couch. "It's hard to believe this is nearly two hundred years old. You don't want to try to sell it?"

"We should just burn it in the fireplace," Anna said. "Get rid of the evidence."

"I knew we should have turned off that prison show," Bobby said flippantly.

Anna opened the refrigerator again, pulled out a bowl of blueberries, and dumped them in the pancake batter. Then she greased the frying pan.

Two minutes later they were sitting down to steaming plates of pancakes and freshly brewed cups of tea. They had become avid tea drinkers since they bought the cottage.

"These look like the best pancakes you've ever made," Bobby teased, trying to lighten the atmosphere, as he smothered them with butter and syrup. Like an actor in a commercial he broke off a piece of pancake with his fork, placed it in his mouth, and with an exaggerated expression of delight, bit down hard.

"Owwww!" he cried.

"What?" Anna yelled.

Bobby reached into his mouth and pulled out a small pebble. His mouth agape, a cap on one of his front teeth fell out and landed on his plate, making a slight tinkling sound before it slid into the syrup. Now he really started screaming. "Owwww! He picked up the cap. "It's cracked! And the air is hitting my tooth. It's so *sensitive!*"

"Oh my God!" Anna cried, leaning in toward him. "That's not a tooth anymore. It looks like a fang! They shaved it down to a stub! We've got to get you to a dentist!"

"Where did that pebble come from?" Bobby screamed, holding his finger to his mouth.

"I don't know. It might have been mixed in with the blueberries."

May Reilly's tablecloth was across the room. And somewhere out there May Reilly was smiling.

13

Regan's parents, Nora—a best-selling suspense novelist—and Luke—owner of three funeral homes in New Jersey—were finishing up a late lunch at Neary's, an Irish pub on East Fifty-seventh Street in New York City, owned by their dear friend Jimmy Neary. Jimmy was the consummate host to everyone who walked through the door. He had emigrated from Ireland more than fifty years ago and eventually opened his restaurant, a place that became known for its convivial atmosphere and delicious comfort food.

It was a beautiful spring afternoon. Two of Luke's cousins, Don and Chris Reilly, and their wives, Helen and Marianne, were his and Nora's guests for lunch. They had come to Regan and Jack's wedding and stayed in New York for a few extra days to shop, take in a show, and just enjoy themselves. Tomorrow they were heading home. Don and Helen lived in Philadelphia, and Chris and Marianne had retired to Naples, Florida.

Relaxing on the leather banquette at a corner table, they were talking about all the Reilly relatives who had been at the wedding and joking about the week Regan had had before her big day, when her wedding dress had been stolen.

"She deserves a rest. Have you heard from her?" Helen asked.

"No news is good news!" Luke said, holding up his hand. "I know Nora would love to talk to Regan, but she's in good hands with Jack."

"He's a doll," Marianne said. "I have to find one like him for our Susan."

"I thank God for him every night," Nora said with a laugh as she reached into her purse for a tissue.

"You don't have to get all choked up about it," Luke commented.

"I'm not," Nora said, rolling her eyes. Her

purse open, she could hear her cell phone begin to ring. "Normally I wouldn't answer my phone in a restaurant," she said, "but I'll just take a peek to see if it's Regan." She looked down. "The caller ID says it's restricted. I'll answer quickly, and if it's not Regan, I'll tell the person I'll call back." She grabbed the phone, turned her head toward the wall, and cupped her free ear with her hand. "Hello," she said, trying to keep her voice down.

"Mom!"

"Regan! How are you?"

"I always knew the Irish were psychic," Don said as he leaned back in his chair. "Regan must have known we were talking about her."

"Maybe I'm the psychic one," Helen whispered. "I just asked if she had called.

"We're fine," Regan told her mother. "I wanted to let you know what was going on in case you heard about what happened from somebody else."

"Heard about what?" Nora asked quickly.

"First of all, there was a fire last night at Hennessy Castle—"

"Good Lord!"

Regan filled Nora in on what had happened since they arrived at the castle, but she didn't mention her four-in-the-morning sighting. "We're on our way to Galway now. We'll be at Gerard's house later this afternoon. . . . Mom, I'm losing reception. Don't worry. I'll talk to you soon. I wish I could say hi to Dad—" The connection was lost.

"Regan?" Nora said hopefully. But there was only silence at the other end. She closed her phone.

"Didn't she want to say hello to dear old dad?" Luke asked. "My hand still hurts from writing out the check for that reception."

The others laughed.

"After Maura got married, my hand had to be wrapped in ice," Don said with a grimace as he flexed his fingers.

It's hard to get a word in edgewise with this group, Nora thought fondly. "Regan did want to talk to you," she told Luke. "Her phone lost reception."

"They're out in the middle of the country, aren't they?" Marianne asked.

"Yes, and you won't believe what's already happened . . ." Nora began.

Jimmy Neary, who had known Regan since she was a child, approached the table. "So, Nora, that was Regan on the phone, was it? How's your girl doing over in my homeland?" he asked, his tone amused, his brogue lilting. "She must be having a wonderful time."

"Jimmy, if you want to hear this, you'd better have a seat."

"What happened?" he asked excitedly, reaching for a chair from the next table without even turning his head.

Nora told the tale. "So it's turned into a working honeymoon."

"Oh my word," Jimmy said, his face astonished. "How do you suppose those two thieves knew they were going to be there?"

Nora looked at the three Reilly men. "They have no idea, but cousin Gerard is going to help them in Galway."

Don laughed. "If anyone knows Galway, Gerard does. Don't you agree, Luke?"

"Naturally."

"Gerard is a lovely guy," Marianne said. "When we visited Ireland, he showed us all around. He knows everyone. It's like he's the mayor, and he does have the gift of gab."

Luke's face grew serious for a moment. "Regan sounds okay, doesn't she?"

"Yes," Nora quickly assured him. "Up until now this Jane and John Doe have been strictly jewel thieves. It seems they intended for the fire they set to be discovered before it got too bad. But instead of relaxing at the castle, Regan and Jack are on their way to Galway right now to see what they can find out."

Luke felt a little relieved. But the expression on Nora's face told him she was holding something back. "Nora, what else did Regan tell you?"

Nora raised her eyebrows. "The woman who made the tablecloth two hundred years ago is reputed to haunt Hennessy Castle."

"Every castle needs a ghost!" Chris pronounced. "It adds to the mystique."

Nora's expression could have given Mona Lisa a run for her money. "The ghost's family name is Reilly."

For a brief moment the group was speechless.

A very brief moment.

Chris lifted his glass. "Which means she must be charming! Let's toast to the ghost Reilly. What's her first name?"

"May."

"May May get her tablecloth back so she can rest in peace, and may Regan and Jack quickly return to enjoying their honeymoon as it should be enjoyed."

Nora smiled as they clinked their nearly empty glasses, but she was uneasy. Who knew what Jane and John Doe might pull if they knew Jack was closing in on them? Why couldn't Regan and Jack just honey-moon in peace?

Luke put his hand on Nora's. "Don't worry, Hon. Regan and Jack will be fine."

"Thanks, Sweetie. I know they will."

14

Regan flipped the phone closed. "Tune in to-morrow," she muttered.

"Your mother sound all right?" Jack asked.

"I'm sure she's not thrilled with what I just told her, but she's used to these calls by now."

Jack smiled. "She doesn't worry as much as she once did now that you're with me."

It was no secret how much Nora loved Jack. "She's created a monster," Regan said with mock frustration.

Regan and Jack were in a small rental car, heading to Galway. Before leaving the castle they had spoken to Liam again to find out more information about the road race.

"There are loads of runners and several races every year in Galway," Liam had said. "This one was a little different. It was more of what you would call a fun run. Not so serious. The guy who started it, Rory Donovan, owns a little gym called Get in Shape. His goal in life is to get people off their behinds. In Galway he's known as the Coach. I'm sure he wouldn't mind talking to you."

Regan had immediately called the gym and left a message for Rory. She was assured by the girl who answered that he'd call back as soon as he finished a workout "with some old fella."

The phone was still in Regan's hand when it rang again. "What did we do before these were invented?" she asked as she opened the cell again and answered.

"Rory Donovan here, returning your call."

"Thanks for calling back." Regan explained the situation to him.

"So you think a couple of thieves ran in my race, do you?" Rory asked. His tone was friendly and inquisitive. "At least they're into fitness. It's *very* important."

"That's one way of looking at it," Regan replied, "but we prefer that they get their exercise in a prison yard."

Rory laughed. "I'm sure you do. Some prisoners really get into shape when they're in jail. They have the time, and exercise relieves their stress. My goal is to make people in the outside world get in shape. I show them how, but they have to make the time!"

"You're right," Regan agreed, not quite believing that she was discussing the exercise habits of prisoners. "Mr. Donovan, if you don't mind—"

"Rory. I'm not fancy. I'm not stuffy. I'm just Rory."

"Okay, Rory. My husband and I want to look into the possibility that the couple we are looking for did in fact participate in that race. They might even be in Galway as we speak. We were wondering if we could meet with you for a few minutes and ask you some questions about the race."

"Certainly. That race is my pride and joy! Last year was the first Fun Run we had. Made a few mistakes, but we'll correct them this year. We didn't have enough tea and sandwiches at the finish line."

Regan felt herself nodding. "Uh-huh. So when would be a good time for us to meet with you?"

"Can you be here in about an hour?"

"Perfect," Regan said quickly. "Thanks so much. What's the address?" She grabbed a small notebook from her purse and wrote down the directions. "We'll see you soon." She hung up. "The Coach is really into fitness."

Jack steered the car around a bend and quickly came to a stop. A farmer wearing knee-high rubber boots was herding several cows across the narrow road. His weathered face was a testimony to his years of working outdoors. He gave a slight wave but obviously didn't feel the need to encourage his plodding bovines to pick up the pace.

"Don't worry about it, pal," Jack muttered under his breath as he waved back. "We're in no hurry."

"The cow crossing is the country's version of a red light," Regan noted with a grin.

"A long red light," Jack said as one cow after another moseyed across the road.

Regan glanced over at a small cottage. The front door was just feet from the side of the road. Lace curtains framed the front window. Lace is so beautiful, Regan thought. It has certainly never gone out of style in Ireland. What was it about the pretty and delicate fabric that made it so timeless? she wondered. And how ironic that lacemaking became popular in Ireland as a way for women to make money during the blight of the potato famine. May Reilly made the Hennessy Castle tablecloth more than twenty years before that.

If only we had taken a minute yesterday to go up and look at May Reilly's handiwork.

The final cow in the procession waddled in front of their car.

"Hallelujah," Jack declared as he stepped on the gas.

It wasn't raining, but the skies were gray and the cloud cover was low. They drove past endless fields of green. Stone cottages and farmhouses dotted the landscape. In the blink of an eye they passed through a tiny village where there were three people out on the street. A minute later they were once again in the middle of green fields.

Finally the road signs indicated that they were getting close to Galway, a medieval town that had recently undergone an unprecedented revival. Galway was now Ireland's cultural capital. Students from the university added to the growing population, along with the young professionals who were attracted by the Irish theater, music, dance, sporting events, and wealth of pubs. Both laidback and bustling, it was said that when walking down the cobblestone streets of Galway, the noise one heard was a combination of talk and music.

Rory had told Regan that the gym was several blocks outside the center of Galway. Just after one o'clock, Regan and Jack spotted a small, nondescript gray building standing alone with a sign above the front door that read GET IN SHAPE. They pulled into the gravel parking lot.

"Let's find out what Coach Rory has to tell us," Jack said as he got out of the car.

A glass door opened onto a small reception area that could best be described as minimalist. A young girl with spiked pink hair, heavy black eyeliner, and numerous bracelets on each wrist greeted them from behind a desk. "Are you interested in a membership?" she asked, a nail file poised in her hand.

"No," Jack answered. "We have an appointment with Rory Donovan."

The receptionist didn't seem the least bit disappointed that they weren't potential members. "Go through the door there," she pointed with her file. "He's in the gym somewhere."

"Thank you."

The gym was small and earthy. It reminded Regan of those grungy gyms in boxing movies. According to Hollywood, you couldn't train to be a champ in a well-lit, pastel-colored, carpeted health club. The gray walls and old wooden floor made Regan think of the gym in her elementary school. The equipment was basic; cardio machines lined one end of the room, and weight machines were located at the other. A full-length mirror covered one wall. There were a dozen people working out, none of them hard-bodied or attired in flashy workout clothes.

Regan liked it. Something about the place felt real. And the room had an energizing smell.

A tall man in shorts and a T-shirt was adjusting the weight on a machine for a guy who looked clueless. "Do a set of eight, rest, and then do it again," he advised.

"Thanks, Coach."

"That's our guy," Jack said to Regan in a low voice.

Spotting Regan and Jack, he hurried over and extended his hand. He was in his mid-forties and had shoulder-length wavy brown hair and intense green eyes. He was wiry, but the muscles in his arms and legs were highly developed like Popeye's. "I'm Rory Donovan. We can talk in my office."

Regan and Jack followed him through a door into a tiny windowless room with a metal desk. Papers were strewn every-where, as were framed pictures of runners competing in what was obviously the Fun Run. A large framed cartoon of exhausted runners piling on top of one another at the finish line of a race hung behind the desk. A zaftig red-headed old lady in the crowd of spectators was leaning over, daintily dab-bing one of their foreheads with her lace handkerchief.

"Is that the decal?" Regan asked as Rory unfolded a couple of chairs for them to sit on.

"Yes. Isn't that too funny?" he asked as he paused, leaned his body to one side, and raised an eyebrow.

"It's very clever," Regan agreed.

"Too funny," he repeated as he finished unfolding the chairs. "I advertised a contest in the newspaper. Said I'd pay two hundred euros for the best logo for the race. A woman sent that in. I never met her." He pointed to an oil painting on the back wall. "She sent me that as a gift after I sent her the check.

She was so happy to have won the contest, but she didn't want any publicity at all. I honored her wishes."

Regan and Jack turned and were struck by an unusual, eye-catching painting that portrayed a misty Irish landscape of rolling hills, a thatched-roof cottage off in the distance, and three cows in the field gathered under a lace umbrella.

"She's good," Regan said. "The landscape is gorgeous and ethereal almost, but the painting is so whimsical."

"I told her that lace umbrella was too funny. I had to laugh, just had to. I wanted to have a show of her paintings here at the gym, but she said no way." He sat at his desk. "Sit down, please."

"Thank you," Regan said as she and Jack took their seats. "This gym is yours?" she asked.

Rory nodded. "I was in the business world in Dublin until I had a heart attack three years ago, age forty-two. I weighed sixty pounds more than I do now. Sixty. That was some wake-up call. I quit my job, moved to Galway, started working out and running, and decided I should help other people get

in shape. I know what it's like to almost drop
dead."

"That is a wakeup call," Regan agreed.

"We both work out at least three times a
week," Jack said dutifully.

"I can tell," Rory commented.

Another detective in the room, Regan
thought.

"People are afraid to get started, or they
don't feel the motivation until something
happens as it did to me. I want to make it
easy for people to start exercising. I didn't
want a gym that would be intimidating. You
know the kind—where you walk in and
everyone looks as if they grew up on Muscle
Beach. Most out-of-shape people turn
around and head for the pub. I purposely
made this gym look the way it does. Kind of
like where Rocky worked out before his first
big match."

Bingo, Regan thought. "Tell us about the
Fun Run," she coaxed.

Rory's smile was crooked. He nodded
with pleasure. "I can't believe we pulled it off.
There are a lot of road races around here
now. A lot of serious runners. I wanted a race
that would be like this gym—relaxed. I

scheduled it for the weekend of the New York Marathon. The hard-core runners would be in New York. I told people who had never been in a race that ours was the first step on the way to running in the marathon. That's why I came up with the idea of having a light-hearted logo. The problem is I can't draw. Hence the contest."

Jack leaned forward. "How many people were in your race?"

"Four hundred and forty-seven, give or take a few."

"Were they all registered?"

"The vast majority were. Some even signed up that morning just before the race. But then others joined the race as it was in progress. We didn't want to be too strict with them because the idea was to encourage people to get out and run. But one thing is for sure. We gave decals only to people who were wearing a number and were registered. We barely had enough. I should have ordered more!"

Regan's pulse quickened. "That's great news," she said.

"Can we get a list of the people who were in the race?" Jack asked.

"I don't see why not." He looked at Jack. "This couple holds a grudge against you, huh?'

Jack gestured with his right hand. "Yes, I suppose they do."

"They must be Irish," Rory laughed. "Let me print out that list." He logged onto his computer, found the file, and printed out three copies. He handed one each to Regan and Jack.

"I've gotten to know a lot of the people on this list, and if any of them turn out to be international jewel thieves, I'll eat my hat."

"Jane and John Doe are both probably in their forties," Jack said. "We could start by eliminating anyone on this list who is very young or much older."

"Let's see," Rory said. "Colleen Adams. You can cross her out. She's about twenty-five. She had a baby and couldn't lose the weight, so she joined our race and ran pushing her baby's pram. It was too funny. That girl is looking good now. She's down ten kilos since the race."

This could take all day, Regan thought.

"Billy McFadden," Rory continued. "He's a young whippersnapper about twenty. At the

beginning of the race he slapped his unath-
letic friend on the arse to get him started,
then sprinted out of sight. A real showoff."

Regan could tell Jack was trying his best
to be patient.

"If we could just quickly go through the
list," Jack said gently. "The Does are an
average-looking couple, probably in their forties. They're masters of disguise, so we don't
even know what color hair either of them had
when they ran the race or what they might
have done to change their appearance. They
could have paraded around that day as older
people for all we know. I see some of the
same last names here. Can we check to see
if any of these people are married or have
the same address?

Twenty minutes later they had narrowed
the list down to five couples whom Rory did
not know personally and who had registered
the morning of the race. He tapped the keys
on his computer. "One of the couples signed
up at the very last minute, but their signatures were indecipherable," he said. "They
didn't give their address." He looked up. "The
race was about to begin, and people were in
a hurry to get to the starting line."

"That might have been them," Jack said,

obviously disappointed. "They wouldn't have wanted to give you their names. What can you tell us about the other four couples who signed up at the last minute?"

Again Rory tapped the keys of his computer. "One couple was staying at the Galway Bay Hotel."

"That could have been them," Regan said quickly. "What are their names?"

"Sheila and Brian O'Shea."

"Sheila and Brian O'Shea?" Jack and Regan said at once.

Rory looked up. "You know them?"

"There's a couple staying up at the Hennessy Castle named Sheila and Brian O'Shea. We met them last night when we had to leave the hotel because of the fire. They said they live in the States and have an Irish memorabilia business. It couldn't be them," Regan said.

"We saw them this morning," Jack told Rory. "Jane and John Doe had already checked out." He turned to Regan. "We'll have to talk to them."

"And the other three couples?" Regan asked Rory.

"None of them gave addresses. But I'll print out their names for you. Donna and Eamonn Byrne, Josie and Joe Cullen, and Linda and Brad Thompson."

"They could have been tourists as well," Regan said. "At least it gives us something to start with. Who was signing the runners in that day? Maybe we can talk to them and see if they remember anything about these people."

"Clara was in charge of that."

"Who's Clara?" Regan asked.

"The girl at the front desk."

Oh, great, Regan thought. I'm sure she'll be a fountain of information. "We'll talk to her on the way out," she said. "And we're visiting my cousin Gerard Reilly today. He has a radio show here in Galway—"

"Gerard Reilly!" Rory said. "Of course I've met him. He has the late-night radio show. I've been trying to get him into the gym for ages, but he's stubborn. He needs to work out!"

"Oh," Regan said, concern in her voice. "I haven't seen him in several years."

"He looks all right," Rory said quickly, "but he admitted he doesn't exercise much. Tell him to come and see me."

"I will," Regan promised. "What I was going to suggest is that we go over this list with him."

"I'm sorry if I wasn't helpful enough."

"You were!" Regan insisted. "Having this list is terrific."

"You've been a great help," Jack acknowledged, handing Rory his card with their cell phone number. "We'll probably call you again, but if there's anything you can think of, anything unusual you remember about anyone who was in the race, please let us know. We both can't thank you enough. You've been a great help to us already."

As Regan and Jack started to walk out of his office, Regan turned. "Rory, there is one more thing. You don't by any chance have an extra decal, do you?"

Rory's face lit up as he pulled open his desk drawer. "I certainly do!" He handed it over. "Isn't it just too funny?"

15

Margaret and Brian raced over to Sheila who was sprawled on the cold stone floor, her eyes closed. Margaret bent down and pulled one of Sheila's eyes open. "You'll be fine, and you know it," she said with a scowl. "I'll make you a cup of tea, then I want the two of you out of here. It'll be bad luck for me if I don't at least show you a little Irish hospitality." She hoisted herself to her feet and headed to the kitchen.

Brian was kneeling next to Sheila, holding her hand. He leaned down and whispered in her ear, "You were better in the fifth grade play. We're going to have to try a different strategy." He pulled her to her feet.

"I do feel woozy," she protested as she stood up and sought to regain her balance.

"Baby, my stomach's killing me," Brian said mournfully, patting his midsection with his large right hand that still sported the ring he had been awarded for playing on a winning college football team.

"Can't I *ever* feel sick without you feeling sick, too?" Sheila asked impatiently as she took in her surroundings. The cottage was fairly dark with old stone walls, simple furnishings, and several horseshoes hanging on the wall. The hearth where the paintings met their demise seemed unusually large. The fire was dying down, having devoured the artwork, and the room felt chilly. A small television set was resting on a table against one wall. It looked exactly like the rural cottage living rooms you see in picture books about Ireland. "I need to sit down," Sheila said.

They sat together on the narrow couch. Both of them were trying not to freak out. They had poured all the money Dermot had given them into Sheila's fledgling Irish memorabilia business. They had a warehouse outside of Phoenix packed full of key chains, trinkets, and china plates bearing every Irish name you could think of. And their hoped-for Saint Patrick's Day spike in sales had never happened.

Brian was secretly blaming Sheila. They had put all their money into the business *she* started.

Sheila thought that if Brian had been truthful on the night of the fund-raiser and not lied about where they got the painting, they wouldn't be in this mess.

A few minutes later, Margaret was back in the room, mumbling to herself as she carried a tray containing a teapot, three cups and saucers, teaspoons, sugar, and milk.

"You are so kind," Sheila said feebly. "I was so upset."

"*You're* upset?" Margaret spat as she poured their tea. "I gave you back your money. What's the big deal? You don't have the ghost of May Reilly after you."

We'll have the real-life Dermot Finnegan after us, Brian thought. No ghost could be worse.

"May Reilly?" Sheila said. "Why is May Reilly mad at you?"

"It's my fault her tablecloth was stolen!"

"What?" Brian asked. "When was it stolen?"

"Where have you two been? Under a rock? Weren't you at Hennessy Castle this morning?"

"We got up and left early. There was a lot of commotion, but we didn't stop to see what was going on." Brian paused. "We were so excited about picking up the paintings."

"Don't aggravate me!" Margaret said as she slurped her tea. "I'm in charge of keeping that memorabilia room in shipshape. Late yesterday afternoon I noticed that the lock on the door was a little loose. I should have reported it. When they closed up the room last night, they didn't notice, I guess. Then sometime during the night the tablecloth was stolen. Probably around the same time I dreamt a tooth fell out of my head."

"You had a bad dream?" Sheila asked sympathetically.

"Bad dream? If you dream a tooth falls out of your head, it means you're about to die— or someone close to you is about to die. When I went to work this morning and realized the tablecloth was stolen, I knew it meant me! May Reilly is going to make sure I die soon."

"I'm sure she wouldn't do that," Sheila said.

"How do you know? She's mad at me. I modeled the lace design in my paintings after the design on her tablecloth."

"You did?"

"You saw her tablecloth at the castle. Didn't you notice that the design was exactly the same in the painting I gave you?"

"No. All we noticed was how beautiful the painting was," Brian explained. His stomach was really hurting.

"You didn't look closely then. I thought you were crazy about that painting! The lace in my paintings has little castles on it, not your usual shamrocks or flowers. That's what May had on her tablecloth. She created the design especially for Hennessy Castle. My mother told me I should never have taken a job there!"

"We didn't notice because there's so much to love about your work—" Sheila began.

"The fairies blessed May with talent. I tried to take a little piece of it and call it my own. I shouldn't have done that. It's stealing! Maybe not exactly like taking something out of her hands, but I never gave May credit for what she created! And the dead are very possessive of what was theirs," Margaret said vehemently. "They come back to claim it!"

Brian swallowed hard. "I wouldn't say what you did was exactly stealing," he said as if to convince himself.

"Yes, it is! It'll be a cold day in hell before I pick up another paintbrush!"

"But Margaret," Sheila said, "the fairies have blessed you with incredible talent. You won that decal contest. You're an artist. It's a sin if you don't put your God-given talents to work."

"My husband didn't think I was any good."

"He's dead now, isn't he? Sheila asked.

"Five years next Tuesday."

"Then you don't have to listen to him anymore. And he was wrong. You are a wonderful artist. You should continue painting."

Brian had aced Problem Solving 101 in college. What he really wanted to do was strangle this woman. But he didn't need to have taken that class to know that that wasn't a solution for this mess. He had to either get Margaret to paint new paintings or find out how many other canvases were hanging on people's kitchen walls that they could somehow get their hands on. He leaned forward and clasped his hands together earnestly. He remembered that communication was the key to problem solving.

"A friend of yours just cooked us breakfast," he said softly to Margaret.

"Who?" Margaret asked, adding more sugar to her tea.

"Philomena."

"You ate at Philomena's?"

"The pharmacist sent us there. Philomena cooked us breakfast, and her grandson interviewed us for a school project."

"That kid is a pest."

Sheila laughed. "We noticed your painting on the wall, and Philomena just adores it."

Brian interrupted, putting his hand on Sheila's so he wouldn't seem so rude. "Did you give paintings to other friends?"

"I gave out eight paintings as presents. I'm sorry to say that every single one of them has May Reilly's design in it. Everything I painted, I gave away." She pointed to the charred ruins in the fireplace. "This was the only time I had so much art of mine piled up in my house, and quite frankly I was embarrassed."

Pushing back an urge to choke the woman, Brian allowed himself to feel slightly optimistic. If they could just get those paintings, then maybe everything would be okay. Heck, if they got all eight, they'd be able to make a little extra cash on the side. They had to deliver only seven paintings to Dermot.

"Should you try to get those other paintings back?" he asked, treading lightly. "To stop May's curse?"

"I gave them to *friends*. I'd look like a fool asking for them back now."

"But couldn't those paintings bring bad luck to their owners?" Brian asked with the expression of an altar boy. "You say that the dead are possessive. Maybe we should get them back. For May. Then we'll figure out something special to do with the paintings that would make May happy. I don't think she wanted you to destroy your beautiful art. We just want to help you."

"Why?" Margaret asked suspiciously.

"Because you seem so . . . so . . ." Brian's voice broke. "You remind me so much of my aunt Eileen. She was such a talented dancer. My uncle Bernie had two left feet. He didn't dance, and he never wanted her to dance without him." Brian started to cry. "It was so tragic. She loved to dance, but after she married him, she never got the chance. What a waste." Tears rolled down his cheeks.

I can't believe this, Sheila thought. I always knew he was a frustrated actor, but I didn't know how convincing he could be.

"Sheila," Brian said, barely able to get the words out, "do you remember Aunt Eileen?" He sobbed again, but this time it sounded like a hiccup.

"Yes," Sheila said, lying through her teeth. Brian didn't have an aunt Eileen. "I was there when she died." Looking over at Margaret, Sheila continued, "On her deathbed she said, 'When I see Uncle Bernie up in heaven, I hope he'll finally have learned to dance.' I told her that she'll be dancing with the angels."

Margaret's eyes welled up. "She forgave him then."

Brian nodded gravely as he wiped tears from his cheeks with his meaty hand. "She forgave him for all those years where she had to sit on the sidelines at family weddings because he didn't want her to dance."

"I suppose I've never forgiven Angus," Margaret said. "Whenever I tried painting, he told me I should be doing something more useful."

"Oh, no," Brian said.

"Umm-hmmm."

"You're lucky that now you have this chance to paint," Sheila said. "Poor Aunt Eileen. By the time Uncle Bernie died, her arthritis was so bad she could barely walk, never mind dance. You're still healthy."

Margaret nodded. "But it doesn't stop May Reilly from being angry at me."

"It could. If we get the paintings with her design back, we'll figure out how to honor her. I bet she doesn't want to be forgotten. And now that the tablecloth is gone, she could be. I think we're all afraid we'll be forgotten when we die. We shouldn't let that happen to May," Sheila said, laying it on thick.

"I don't want those paintings back in this house," Margaret replied sharply.

"Of course not," Brian said, anguish in his tone. "We'll round up all the paintings you gave away, and I promise you it'll all work out. Now, let's put together a list of the names and addresses of all those who are lucky enough to be your friend."

16

"I look like a freak!" Bobby squealed, examining with horror his filed-down tooth in the bathroom mirror. "Where are we going to find a dentist around here?"

"Online—where we find everything," Anna assured him.

She went to the computer, looked up dentists in Galway, and printed out a list. One by one she called them, but she wasn't having much luck.

"The doctor doesn't have any free appointments until Friday."

"Sorry, she's booked."

"The dentist is on vacation."

"Have you seen us before? . . . No? . . . We can squeeze you in a week from Wednesday."

Finally, working her way from A to Z, Anna called a Dr. Daniel Sharkey. A woman with a frail voice answered the phone. "Dr. Sharkey's smile center."

"Hello," Anna said. "I wonder if you could possibly help us—"

"Hold on a second."

Anna could hear a television in the background. She waited.

"Okay," the woman said, finally resuming their conversation. "What did you want?"

"We're visiting Ireland. My husband was eating blueberry pancakes when . . ."

At the other end of the phone, the woman sighed as she listened to Anna's tale of woe. When Anna was finished, the woman again told her to hold on.

A jarring thud sounded in Anna's ear. The woman had obviously dropped the phone. Anna tapped her foot impatiently, hoping she wouldn't be disconnected. This wasn't what she was used to. Bobby's caps had been done in Los Angeles by an expensive cosmetic dentist, Dr. Favorman, who tended to the mouths of numerous celebrities. His office had a private entrance for his famous clients, which Bobby discovered, of course, and took advantage of on every visit. As long as Dr. Favorman was paid the big bucks, he was happy. Thankfully, his patients' private lives didn't interest him, and his receptionist was always cheerful and courteous.

"I'm back," the voice at the other end of the phone rasped. "You have his X-rays?"

No, you idiot, Anna wanted to shout. Why would we have his dental records with us in Ireland? But she was polite. "Unfortunately, we don't."

"Pity. Dr. Sharkey's X-ray machine is on the fritz. Come on in, but be prepared to wait. He has an appointment with a patient that hadn't been to the dentist in twenty years until last week when he graced us with his presence." She laughed ruefully. "He'd never flossed in his life. And once you start with gum disease, it can kill you. Travels to your heart."

This doesn't sound promising, Anna thought, but she was desperate. Bobby would be impossible to live with until that fang was covered. "Thank you," she said. "We should be there within the hour."

They dressed in blue jeans and sweaters,

grabbed their all-weather coats, which was the optimistic way to describe a raincoat in Ireland, locked up the house, and went out to the car.

"You'd better drive," Bobby whimpered. He had put Vaseline around his stub, but it was sensitive to cold air. "I can't believe how sore it feels."

The high from having ruined Jack Reilly's honeymoon had been wiped out by a pebble.

"Don't worry," Anna said soothingly. "We'll get you a new cap, and you'll be fine." I hope, she thought. With the little enthusiasm she could muster. "You look completely different. It's a disguise we'll have to try—going tooth-less," she joked.

"That's not funny," Bobby whined as got in the car, put the seat back, and closed his eyes.

Good, Anna thought. Let him sulk. I'll have some peace. She flicked on the radio to a station that played jazz. Forty-five minutes later, directions in hand, she turned onto Dr. Sharkey's street. Her heart sank. From the look of the old row houses on the block, one wouldn't imagine that Dr. Sharkey had a booming business. If he had any celebrity clients, they certainly didn't need a private entrance because no paparazzi would venture here. The street was dreary and deserted. She located the house where Dr. Sharkey hung his shingle. Under his name was a red smiley-face and the words "The Smile Center." She parked the car.

"Where are we?" Bobby asked, his voice rising as he opened his eyes and sat up. "This doesn't look like Galway."

"I didn't say the dentist's office was exactly in Galway," Anna answered, trying to maintain a positive attitude. "We're *near* Galway."

"But this looks like the dentist's house I went to when I was six years old! My mother said he should only fill potholes. And Dr. Favorman's office in Los Angeles is so plush and nice." Bobby was panicked.

"Do you realize how many dentists I called before I could find anyone to fit you in today? Besides, it's not as if you're getting a root canal or a tooth pulled. He'll just fix you up with a temporary cap. How much can that hurt?"

"A lot."

"If this doesn't work out, we'll find another dentist. We'll drive to Dublin if we have to."

The entrance to the office was on the side of the house. Anna and Bobby walked along the cracked sidewalk to the door, rang the bell, and, as the sign above the bell instructed them, walked right in. The tiny waiting room, with its three orange velour folding chairs, cracked linoleum floor, and drab paneled walls, was ghastly. The sound of a whirring drill pierced the air.

Bobby immediately turned to leave, but Anna grabbed his arm. "I want to go home," he whimpered. "This place even smells exactly like that dentist office I just told you about."

"It'll be okay," Anna promised.

A birdlike woman, who had to be at least eighty, was seated at a makeshift reception desk. Engrossed in a television soap opera and eating mysterious gruel from a tin can, she gave no indication that she was aware of their presence. Anna walked over and rested her purse on the raised Formica countertop above the woman's desk where people presumably forked over the money to be tortured. The "receptionist" remained riveted to the screen as two gorgeous young girls started screaming at each other about a man. One of them tried to slap the other, missed, and in two seconds they were rolling around the floor, scratching, clawing, and pulling each other's hair. In the middle of such high drama, the show cut to a commercial. Soap operas are the same the world over, Anna thought.

The old woman shook her head disapprovingly, mumbled, "He's not worth it, girls," and then looked up at Anna. "Are you here for the cap?" she croaked. Her gray hair was pulled up in a bun, and frameless glasses rested on her pointy nose. Her Irish eyes were unsmiling. She wore a simple maroon jacket over a white blouse, and a garish rainbow pin was attached to her left lapel.

"Yes, we are," Anna answered, anxious to make everything go smoothly. "I love your pin," she lied.

"It's a gift from my son," the woman answered, not a shred of maternal pride in her voice. "Dr. Sharkey is with a patient. I have some forms for you to fill out." She put down her spoon, opened a drawer, then another, and on the third try finally retrieved a clipboard with a cheap pen dangling from it on a ratty piece of string. "Here," she said, handing it to Anna. She then reached over to a shelf on the wall. "And here are the forms."

Anna frowned at the sight of all the questions on the first page. "Do we really have to fill these out? We just want a temporary cap to tide my husband over, and we're paying cash. Our dentist is in the States."

The woman stared up at her. "You're paying cash?"

"Yes."

She waved her hand dismissively. "Just have a seat then." Picking up her spoon, she turned her gaze back to the television.

The folding chairs proved to be as uncomfortable as they looked. Seated next to Bobby, who again had his eyes closed, Anna picked up a dusty magazine from the table next to her. It was dated three years ago. She dropped it back on the table.

The sight of Bobby looking so vulnerable was distressing. She didn't blame him for being a wreck. She certainly wouldn't have wanted to be in his shoes right now. Gently placing her hand on his, she leaned toward him. "Sweetie, we'll do something fun and exciting after this," she said softly, talking to him as if he were a child.

"Like what?" he asked somberly, opening his eyes

"I'll think of something."

The drill, which had mercifully stopped, started up again. *Whirrrrrrr.* Pause.

Whirrrrrrrrrrrr. Pause. *Whirrrrrrrrrrrrrrrrrrrrrrrrrrrrrrrrrrr.*
Bobby squeezed her hand hard.

These walls must be made of cardboard,
Anna thought.

Several excruciating minutes later the door
to the treatment room flew open. A bearded
man with tufts of gray hair spouting from the
sides of his otherwise bald head emerged
with the air of a general triumphant in victory.
"Mother," he said jovially, "let's make another
appointment for Mr. O'Leary, shall we? We
made a lot of progress today. Yes, indeed!"

Mother? No wonder she doesn't have
to worry about customer relations, Anna
thought. But what's even more frightening is
his taste in jewelry.

Mr. O'Leary stumbled out. Big, bulky, and
middle-aged, he was attired in jeans, a red
and black flannel jacket, and work boots.
Watching him walk haltingly to the desk was
like witnessing a baby taking his first steps.
Anna wondered if he was the patient who
hadn't been to a dentist in twenty years. If he
is, I bet it's another twenty before he comes
back, she decided.

Dr. Sharkey turned to Anna and Bobby
and smiled. "Next victim!" he bellowed, then

laughed heartily. "I made you smile, didn't I? Welcome to the smile center! I understand it's the gentleman who is here to see me."

What a nerd this guy is, Anna thought.

Bobby nodded gravely, stood, and followed the cheery Dr. Sharkey into the treatment room. Before the door shut, Anna got a quick glance of a dentist's chair that needed serious reupholstering, a tray lined with sharp metal utensils, and a tank of what she suspected might be nitrous oxide. She turned and watched as O'Leary took his appointment card, tried to locate his pocket but missed twice, and exited as though he'd just downed six beers. That must be nitrous oxide in there, she thought. And judging from Dr. Sharkey's behavior, the tank must have sprung a leak.

Mother Sharkey had switched the TV channel to the news. She poured tea from a thermos as a reporter for a local station gave an update on the fire at Hennessy Castle.

"We just received word from a reliable source that a man and woman working together stole the tablecloth and set the fire, and left a note for Jack Reilly, an American who is head of the Major Case Squad in—"

Anna's heart raced. She was exhilarated. All fears of prison were banished from her mind. This is what she lived for.

"—Reilly is reportedly not happy. He's on his honeymoon, and looking for a couple known as Jane and John Doe is not the way he wanted to spend time with his new bride."

Too bad, Anna thought.

"—The only description given of this couple is that they are average-looking—average height, average weight, no unusual characteristics. It's easy for them to slip in and out of disguises and blend into crowds because they are so very average."

The nerve of them, Anna mused. I feel pretty—like Maria in *West Side Story.*

"They were disguised as an elderly couple, but now who knows what appearance they've taken on? Whatever it is, you can be sure they don't want to attract attention."

That's why we're in this dump, Anna thought. A missing front tooth will most likely elicit a fair share of double takes.

"Anyone who has any leads, please call the garda."

Uh-oh.

"Would you like to take a look at the newspaper?" Mother Sharkey asked sweetly.

Anna almost jumped. She was so startled to hear the receptionist speak to her. And the woman's timing seemed suspect. "Thank you, I would." She went over and retrieved a local Galway paper from the older woman's outstretched hand.

Mother Sharkey snapped off the television. "I'm going into the house for a few minutes. If you'll excuse me . . ." She didn't wait for an answer, exiting through a door behind her desk, clutching the thermos bottle.

For a moment Anna panicked. Could this suddenly friendly woman be calling the garda about them? No. Anna realized she was being paranoid. Mother Sharkey is probably filling that thermos with whiskey. Anna glanced down and was immediately riveted by the headline on the front page of the paper.

CLADDAGH RINGS FOUND IN GALWAY
BASEMENT AUTHENTICATED AS ORIGINALS!
AUCTION EXPECTED TO FETCH A TIDY SUM!

Claddagh rings? Anna remembered that a couple of her Irish American friends in New York wore Claddagh rings. Her eyes widened as she skimmed the article.

Claddagh rings originated over three hundred years ago in Claddagh, a little fishing village in Galway. Legend has it that a Richard Joyce, who was from one of the original family tribes in Galway, had been kidnapped by pirates when he was on a trip to the West Indies. He was taken to Algiers where he was sold as a slave to a goldsmith who taught him the trade. Joyce proved to be very adept. In 1689, when King William III of England demanded the release of British slaves from Algiers, the goldsmith begged Joyce to stay, marry his daughter, and assume half his fortune. But Richard refused.

What an idiot, Anna thought as she continued reading.

Joyce returned to Galway where he found his true love still unmarried and waiting for him. He presented her with a ring whose design featured two hands holding a heart topped with a crown. The couple married, and together they lovingly made copies of her ring for the next forty years. Jewelers in Ireland and now the world over have been making Claddagh rings ever since.

The announcement that Joyce's five recently discovered rings will be available for sale is cause for excitement. The rings bear his stamp and are sure to fetch untold sums when they are put up for auction in Galway on Friday, April 15.

That's this Friday, Anna thought. Then she looked at the date on the paper. It was a week old. She continued to read:

A cocktail party will be held at the Galway Arts Center where the rings will be on display before the 8 P.M. auction. The owner of the house where the rings were found plans to give half the proceeds from the sale of the rings to various Irish charities.

Not if I can help it, Anna thought excitedly. We're going to steal those rings and sell them for a fortune on the black market. How many wealthy Irish around the world would love to have an original Claddagh ring? Wait until Bobby hears this! He's bored sitting around the cottage, and so am I. We need to do something to make us feel alive. I told him I'd find something fun. I just hope this wacky dentist can make a decent-looking cap for him.

She could hear Bobby through the wall, laughing and talking loudly. That nitrous must be starting to affect him. She cocked her head to listen.

"We love to travel, just love it. We go all over. *Henh, henh, henh. Henh, henh.* Yes, we're American. That's your mother working out there, huh? My wife was admiring her pin. You picked it out? Super! My wife loves nice jewelry, too. I mean she really likes nice jewelry. I mean really, really, really likes jewelry. *Henh, henh, henh, henh, henh, henh.*"

Anna jumped up and yanked open the door to the treatment room. Dr. Sharkey looked at her with a shocked expression. Bobby's face was covered with a mask, and, not surprisingly, he didn't budge.

"Is anything wrong?" Dr. Sharkey asked.

"I heard my husband laughing. He shouldn't have that gas. He has a little heart problem," Anna said, gesturing toward her chest.

"A heart problem? He didn't tell me that. That's why we want you to fill out those awful forms!" Dr. Sharkey turned, shut off the gas, and then tapped Bobby on the shoulder. "You're a scoundrel!"

"But—*henh, henh.*"

"Sweetie, no gas," Anna said firmly.

"But I—"

"No."

"I won't let him have any more of the funny stuff," Dr. Sharkey promised. "I'll tell him jokes to make him laugh. Now, if you'll go back to the waiting room, I'll have him looking gorgeous in no time."

Average, Anna thought. Just make him look average.

17

Regan and Jack stopped to talk to Clara on the way out of the Get in Shape gym. They showed her the list of people who had signed up at the last minute for the Fun Run in November.

"I don't know any of them," Clara said, shaking her head and tugging on one of her many earrings.

"Rory told us that one couple signed up right before the race started and signed a registration form, but their handwriting was so bad, he couldn't read their names to add them to the final list of runners. Is there any chance you remember them?" Regan asked. "I know it was five months ago," she acknowledged.

"Oh, those two! I remember them." Clara scrunched her nose and started to laugh.

"You remember them?" Jack asked, surprise in his voice.

"For sure. They came running up to the table at the last minute. He signed their names super-fast, paid the money, and they pinned on their numbers. Then they dashed off to the starting line but didn't get far. She tripped on her shoelace and fell. The guy started laughing really hard. I mean, he helped her up, and she was okay. I remember it because his laugh was so weird. A friend was helping me with the registration, and we started cracking up, and the fella started laughing even harder. He thought we were laughing at his wife, but we were laughing at his laugh." She shook her head, smiling at the memory. "My friend and I still joke about his stupid laugh. It's silly, but it's one of those things."

"I understand," Regan said, thinking of how she and her best friend, Kit, still reminisced about some of the memorable characters they had met since college. "What was the laugh like?" she asked.

"I'm not as good as my friend is at it," Clara said. "Maebeth is a perfect mimic."

"Could you try?" Regan asked.

Clara smiled. "Okay. It was—" she scrunched up her face—"Hey, hey, hey. No, wait a minute. It didn't sound like that. It was *hey, hey, hey.*" Clara grimaced. "Wait a second." She picked up the phone and dialed at the speed of sound. "Maebeth, I need for you to do the laugh. . . . I'll explain later. . . . Let me put you on speaker phone."

"Helllllllo," Maebeth said playfully, her Irish lilting voice coming through loud and clear. "Here I ammmmm." She sounded so young and happy.

"Okay, go," Clara ordered. "Do it."

"Henh, henh. Henh, henh, henh."

"That's perfect!" Clara exulted. "Do a couple more."

"Henh, henh. Henh, henh, henh."

The two friends started to guffaw.

"Thanks, Maebeth. I'll ring you later—"

"Wait a minute," Regan interrupted. "Since we have Maebeth on the phone, can we ask you a few more questions?"

"Sure," Clara answered. "Maebeth, some people here need information about the fella with the laugh and his wife."

"Henh, henh, henh, henh," Maebeth continued for good measure. *"Henh, henh, henh, henh—"*

"That's great, Maebeth," Regan said. "Can you give us a description of what they looked like?"

"They were wearing caps and big sunglasses and windbreakers. They both had brown hair and looked as old as my parents. You know, in their forties," Maebeth volunteered. "But unlike my parents you could tell they both worked out a lot. Not an extra kilo on either one of them."

"Anything unusual about them at all?" Jack asked. "Besides the laugh?" he added.

"Isn't the laugh enough?" Clara giggled.

Not really, Regan thought. We're looking for an average middle-aged couple. Male possibly has a distinguishing laugh. We could use more help. "What nationality were they?" Regan asked.

"American," both girls answered.

Jack gave Clara his card. "Thank you, girls, so much. If you remember anything else about those two, or anything unusual about the race, please let us know."

"Sure."

Out in the car, Regan and Jack looked at

each other. "What now?" Regan asked. "Go tell jokes to everyone we meet. Stake out comedy clubs?"

Jack rubbed his eyes. "Call your cousin Gerard. If he knows everything going on in Galway, maybe he can help us with these names."

Twenty minutes later they were walking into Gerard's office at a small radio station in the center of Galway.

18

Back at Hennessy Castle, Neil Buckley was doing his best to cope. Most of the guests had checked out, others had called to cancel their upcoming reservations, and there was no new stove in sight.

The garda had come by to investigate the theft and the fire but had already gone on their way. The owners of the hotel were calling demanding answers, of which he had none. Neil's wife, Felicity, rang him for the third time in two hours.

"Darling, how are you?"

"Since I talked to you last, the press has gotten wind of the note left for Jack Reilly, and it's all over the news. I'm sure he didn't want it announced to the world that these thieves are playing hide and seek with him on his honeymoon."

"I'm afraid I have more bad news."

"What?"

"Your housekeeper, Margaret, is going bonkers."

Neil wanted to put his head on his desk. "I know that. You know I know that. But she's a good housekeeper. Why do you want to discuss it now?"

"She just appeared at the door and asked if I would mind handing over the painting she gave us last year. She was mumbling something about May Reilly and bad luck. She said the design of the lace in the painting is the same as the lace on May's stolen tablecloth. I hadn't noticed, quite frankly. Margaret said she had to get the painting back because it would bring us bad luck."

"Seems as though it already has. What did you do?"

"I gave her the painting, of course. She was acting positively nutty. She said she was going to collect *all* her paintings." Felicity paused. "What else was I supposed to do? I hope you don't mind."

"Believe me, I don't. Did she tie the painting to her bike?" Neil asked wearily. "She insists on bicycling in the rain when she has that old rattletrap her husband drove parked behind her cottage. I'll admit it's not the greatest, but—"

"Actually, she didn't have her bike. I ran to the front window and watched her leave. She walked down the street to where her old car was parked, got in the back, and the car drove off."

"She has a chauffeur now?" Neil asked distractedly.

"It was the oddest thing."

"You didn't see who was driving?"

"No. I wish I had. I'm dying to know who it was."

Neil sighed. "I gave her the day off to go home and calm down. Now she's being driven around to collect her art. Ah, well, if that's what she needs to feel better."

Martin, Neil's assistant, burst into the office. "Good news, Mr. Buckley!" he blurted.

"Just a moment, love," Neil said to his wife. "They're getting a stove for us today?" he asked Martin hopefully.

"No. But the representative of an American businessman, one of those high rollers, just rang us up. His boss read about the auction of the Claddagh rings in Galway this Friday and wants to be there. He is flying over with an entourage. They'd like to book eight of our superior rooms for five nights starting tomorrow."

"Did you tell them we have no stove?"

"Yes, and he doesn't care. The best hotels in Galway are already booked, and this fella wants to play golf around here with his pals."

Relief flooded Neil's body. "I hope you told him yes."

A flash of nervousness crossed Martin's face. "I told him I had to check on availability. Didn't want him to think it was so easy to get all those rooms at Hennessy Castle on a moment's notice—stove or no stove."

"Of course," Neil said, feeling slightly irritated. "Where is he from?"

"Phoenix. He's Irish American—Dermot Finnegan—and his rep said he's very generous to Irish charities. But he also warned me that Mr. Finnegan is *very* demanding and expects first-rate service."

"If Mr. Finnegan doesn't care that we don't have a working stove, how demanding can he be?" Neil asked rhetorically. "Book the reservation."

"The rep does want us to guarantee that Mr. Finnegan will be served a hot breakfast in bed every morning. He requires scrambled eggs, bubbly hot oatmeal, freshly baked brown bread—"

"For God's sake, Martin, get out there and book the reservation before they change their minds!" Neil growled, his face turning red. "I'll get him his oatmeal if I have to set up a campfire out back and carry the tray on my hands and knees to his room!"

"Yes, sir," Martin replied, escaping as quickly as possible.

Neil was breathing hard. "Anything else, dear?" he managed to sputter into the phone.

"Darling, take a deep breath."

"What does it sound like I'm doing?" Neil asked impatiently. "I'm taking so many deep breaths, I might keel over."

"Don't keel over. Things are looking up. Forget I ever mentioned the silly painting."

"I will," Neil said. "Believe me, I will. As long as Margaret Raftery gets herself back to work tomorrow, be it by bike, chauffeur, or on foot, I don't care how crazy or superstitious she acts on her time off."

He wouldn't always feel that way.

19

"One down," Margaret said when she got in the backseat and shut the door. She placed the framed painting on the seat next to her.

"Perfect!" Brian said as he pulled away. "I told you it would be easy. May Reilly is going to be so happy. Who was that anyway?"

"My boss's wife!"

"Your what?" Brian asked, turning around and nearly losing control of the rusty old rattletrap of a car.

"My boss's wife. What's wrong with that?"

"Your boss from Hennessy Castle?" Brian's voice squeaked.

"Yes. I gave them this painting for Christmas."

Sheila looked out the window. She was biting her nail down to the quick.

"Did she ask you many questions about why you wanted the painting back?"

"Not too many. I feel a wee bit insulted she didn't put up more of a fuss about giving it back. I gave it to her with this lovely frame that I specially picked out. It was on sale."

"You didn't say anything about us, did you?

"No. Why would I? You told me not to."

"That's right. Now, is there anyone else who works at Hennessy Castle on the list? Because if there is, I'd like to know."

Margaret shook her head. "I just gave one painting to the boss. Figure I'd butter him up. The rest of us just have a little Christmas grab bag at the employee party. We buy cheap little presents for it. Next year I should put in a coupon for one of your mugs."

"Our mugs are high quality," Sheila hissed.

"Whatever," Margaret said, trying to get comfortable in the old car. The backseat was crooked, and a draft was coming through a hole at her feet. "I wanted to go to the Buckleys' house first because I knew Mr. Buckley wouldn't be home yet. I don't need to run into him on my time off. Don't you want to even look at the painting? This one's a beauty if I do say so myself."

Sheila turned around and admired the painting of an old farmhouse with a lace wreath on the door. "It's gorgeous." She turned back to face front.

"I can't wait to examine the painting," Brian said, dripping with sincerity. "But right now it's important I keep my eyes on the road. I've been racking my brain trying to figure what we can do with these paintings that would somehow honor May Reilly."

"I need a cup of tea," Margaret announced.

"Now?" Brian asked.

"Now. We've been in the car forty-five minutes, and I'm down a quart." She chuckled. "That's what my mother used to say when she didn't have a cup of tea at her side."

They were near Galway.

"We'll stop and get you tea," Brian promised. "But first, are you sure that there's no one else living down this way who has one of your paintings?"

Margaret frowned. "I don't know people in these parts." She then snapped her fingers. "Wait a minute! I almost forgot. I gave one to the owner of the gym who judged the contest."

"What contest?"

"The decal contest for the road race you two ran in. Remember when I saw the decal on your dresser, and I told you I designed it? That's what got us started with this mess."

"You gave him one of your paintings?" Brian asked in disbelief.

"Yes. He said he really liked it."

"Where is his gym?"

"Somewhere around Galway. I think it's called Get in Shape."

Sheila pulled out the cell phone, called information, and wrote down the address. "Should we call first?"

"No," Brian said. "Absolutely not."

"This is going to be strange," Margaret said. "I've never been inside a gym in my life."

"Think of May Reilly," Brian urged. "Now what's the address?"

"Wait a minute," Sheila said. "What if this guy has the painting hanging in his house? He probably doesn't have it at the gym."

"He told me he has it hanging proudly in his office," Margaret said. "*He* noticed the use of lace in my work—not like you two."

They drove to the Get in Shape gym and were about to pull into the parking lot when Brian spotted Regan and Jack Reilly coming out the door. "Good God," he muttered as he stepped on the gas.

Judging by the look on Sheila's face, she had seen them, too. Luckily, Margaret hadn't.

"What's the matter?" Margaret sputtered. "That was the place we were looking for."

"We didn't get you your tea yet."

"I want to get this over with—"

"I insist you have your tea first," Brian said. "I absolutely insist."

They found a little deli. Brian ran in and came out with teas for all three of them.

"It's pretty good for city tea," Margaret allowed as she downed the large container in two gulps. "Let's go. If we don't get the painting now, I'm afraid I'll lose the wee bit of nerve I have. Setting foot in a gym for the first time at my age has got to be bad luck."

Brian briefly considered suggesting they not bother with the painting at the gym. It might be too risky. What if the Reillys come back? And if he and Sheila ended up with every painting on the list, they'd have one to spare. But then he realized he wouldn't be able to explain this change of plan to Margaret. In her world, everything was about bad luck or curses.

They drove back to the gym and dropped Margaret off at the entrance to the parking lot. "We'll wait for you down the block by the deli," Brian told her.

"Why can't you just wait for me out front?"

Brian's eyes welled up with tears. "I told you—you remind me of my aunt Eileen. The time I'm sacrificing helping you . . . well, I'm offering it up for her soul. Aunt Eileen believed in doing good and not looking for the glory. Whenever she donated money, she did it anonymously. She'd be so proud of me. . . . If anyone finds out what I'm doing, then I might not help her get out of purgatory. I think she's already made it to heaven, but just in case . . ."

"I understand," Margaret said solemnly. "Have you heard a ringing in your ears?"

"What?" Brian asked, perplexed.

"A ringing in your ears means a friend in purgatory is asking for your prayers. I would think you would know that!" She pushed open the stubborn back door. "I'll meet you down the block in a few minutes."

After Margaret got out of the car, Sheila

stared at Brian. "As Sister Leo used to tell us, God is going to punish you."

"All I know is that if we don't deliver those paintings, we'll definitely be punished by Dermot Finnegan. And that, my dear Sheila, would be hell on earth."

They drove down the block and waited.

20

Jack couldn't believe how much he instantly liked Gerard Reilly. For some reason, after the phone call early this morning, he was sure that spending time with Gerard would be well spent but leaning more toward family obligation than pleasure. But the moment Gerard came out of his office to greet the newlyweds, his charismatic air and big commanding presence made Jack feel a camaraderie he shared with many of his law enforcement colleagues back home.

Dressed in a blue jacket and open-collared shirt, Gerard had a casual yet professional appearance. He was a broad, good-looking man in his early fifties, with salt and pepper hair, dark eyes, and black-framed glasses. "Regan," he said, enveloping her in a hug. "How's my little cousin keepin' herself?"

Regan smiled broadly and kissed him on the cheek. "Your little cousin is now a happily married woman."

Gerard extended his hand. "Jack, it's good to finally meet you. Come into my office. I'm so sorry we couldn't make it to the wedding. My wife's niece was getting married the very same day, you know, and we'd already committed ourselves. It was grand, but we would have loved to be at yours."

"We realized it would have been tough for you to fly over for just a weekend anyway," Regan assured him. "But we wanted you to know you were invited."

"Ah, Regan," Gerard said, "we'd have been there in a heartbeat if not for the other nuptials. Believe me. I might not have seen you many times over the years, but I remember when you were born. I remember when your parents brought you over when you were a little girl, and I remember when you came to visit with that lovely friend of yours. . . . What was her name?"

"Kit."

"That's it, Kit."

"You were here with Kit?" Jack's voice was surprised. "What kind of trouble did you get into then?"

"No trouble, Jack," Regan said quickly, making a face at him. "That's when Kit and I first met. We were juniors in college, spending a semester in England. We visited Ireland for a long weekend and took a train here from Dublin. We stayed a night at Gerard's house."

"I have pictures to prove it," Gerard volunteered. "I'll show you tonight. They were so sweet, Jack. Regan was very interested in the Reilly family history. She had long hair then."

"Jack doesn't need to see those pictures," Regan said with a laugh.

"You were a cute little lass. Now, sit, sit, sit," Gerard said, gesturing to a couch in his office.

The room had a large window overlooking the busy street below. Framed photos of Gerard's family were resting on a shelf behind his desk. He had two sons, both in Dublin—one at university and the other working at a computer software firm. Various awards were hung on the wall heralding Gerard's career as a radio show host.

"We have an empty nest," Gerard told them with a touch of regret. "It's very strange. Louise and I didn't know what to do with ourselves when Timmy went off to Trinity. He'll be back for the summer, which makes us happy. We miss having people around the dinner table. These days we often just go out. That's why Louise is so pleased to cook for you tonight."

"We're looking forward to it," Jack said. "And we hate to bother you when you're at work—"

"You're not bothering me at all. Not a whit. It's lovely to have you here. I'm so sorry that you have those two thieves making trouble for you."

Regan looked puzzled. "How did you know?" When she had called Gerard and asked if they could stop by the radio station, she hadn't said anything about the reason they were already in Galway. And when they had spoken earlier this morning, Regan and Jack were still unaware that the tablecloth had been stolen or that Jane and John Doe were involved.

"Didn't you know?" Gerard asked. "Word's

gotten out that the thieves of the tablecloth left you their calling card."

"Great," Jack said. "I just don't understand how they could have known I was going to be here. We talked to the bellman at the hotel who brought the couple to their room." He told Gerard about Jane and John Doe's history, the decal, and how he and Regan had visited the Get in Shape gym and secured the list of names of people from the Galway race whom Rory did not know personally.

"That Rory has been after me to join the gym."

"He told us," Regan said.

"I suppose I should. But Louise and I often go for walks on the prom."

"The prom?" Regan asked.

"You should check it out. It's a lovely promenade overlooking Galway Bay, just west of here in Salthill. More than a mile-long, it's a wonderful spot for a stroll or a run. There are lots of restaurants and bars where you can stop for a gargle. A lot of people exercise every day on the prom."

"We think Jane and John Doe are athletic. Maybe we should stake it out," Jack said half-jokingly.

"I'd be happy to help you in any way I can,"

Gerard volunteered. "If you like, you can be guests on my show later tonight, and we'll talk about the case. We'll put out an appeal for people to be on the lookout for the two scoundrels. Jack and Regan, you're experienced investigators. Tell my listeners what they can do to help, and I'm sure they will. People in Ireland are known for their exchange of information, shall we say."

"What do you think, Jack?" Regan asked. "Ireland's version of *America's Most Wanted*"?

Jack smiled. "The Does might have left the country by now, but it can't hurt, I suppose. The problem is that we don't have much of a physical description to go on."

"No stone unturned," Regan said. "I think we should try. Gerard, did you know that the stolen tablecloth was made by a woman named May Reilly two hundred years ago? And she reputedly haunts Hennessy Castle?"

"I did, Regan," Gerard answered. "I've been up to Hennessy Castle for several functions over the years. The tablecloth was exquisite, let me tell you. I did a little digging to see if May Reilly is one of our relations, but, alas, she isn't. The people at the castle say she does make her presence known there from time to time. Who knows?

Whether you believe in ghosts or not, we all like a good ghost story, don't we?"

"I can tell you that one of the Hennessy Castle housekeepers definitely believes in ghosts. She was the one who discovered that the tablecloth was gone, and she was very upset. The hotel manager had to send her home, she was so distraught. She was sure that May Reilly would be furious and come back to haunt the castle with a vengeance."

Gerard nodded. "We have a lot of lovely myths and legends in Irish lore and quite a few superstitions. Regan, our great-grandmother would never thread a needle on Sunday because she believed it was bad luck. Can you imagine?"

Regan decided she wouldn't volunteer that she thought she had seen a ghost, maybe even May Reilly. No need for Gerard to question her sanity. At least not yet. She smiled and said lightly, "Well, if May Reilly isn't one of our relatives, maybe she's related to Jack."

"Can't I be related to a friendly ghost?"

"May Reilly is probably very friendly," Regan insisted. "She should have been paid for that tablecloth, and that's why she can't stay away from Hennessy Castle. She's standing up for her rights."

"Money's not going to do her much good now," Gerard reflected. "If she's a friendly ghost, maybe she's standing up for someone else who's being shortchanged. Now, let me take a look at that list of names."

21

"We have a new mission, Robert!" Dermot Finnegan exulted to his long-suffering right-hand man. "You know how I love projects, and this is a winner!" They were in Dermot's palatial bedroom, busy packing Dermot's bags for the trip to Ireland.

After talking to Brian, and fueled by his excitement about the paintings, twice-divorced Dermot had gone online to Google everything having to do with nuns and clois-tered convents. He was hoping to find the secret location of his mysterious painter. As he petted the beloved Maltese sleeping in his lap, the only creature on earth who gave him unconditional love, a challenge even for a dog, he'd been fascinated to find mention of a group of nuns from Valos who had fled their convent and took refuge inside a Greek monastery. Their knitting business had been thrown for a loop, and they were one million dollars in debt. No further details were given.

"Ladies, you should take up painting," he said, chuckling to himself. "It's much more profitable." He looked down at his pet. "Isn't that right, Poochey?"

Poochey seemed to agree, momentarily lifting his head.

Narrowing his search to all things Irish, Dermot had come upon the story of the newly authenticated Claddagh rings and the upcoming auction. A lump had formed in his throat. His mother and father had both worn Claddagh rings as wedding bands. Dermot had cherished the rings after his parents died, keeping them in a special box in his safe. But they'd been stolen in a burglary at his house last year. Thousands in cash and priceless silver had also been taken. But the theft of the rings was what had broken his heart.

He had planned to pass the rings on to his twin grandchildren on their sixteenth birth-

day. These days they made such produc-
tions about sixteenth birthdays, a modern-
day development of which Dermot did not
entirely approve. When he was their age, he
was working two jobs after school. For his
birthday his mother made him his favorite
chocolate cake—and that meant the world
to him. He had decided that if Sean and
Sinead had the Claddagh rings on their fingers, they would always serve as a reminder
to them of their heritage and how hard their
great-grandparents worked to make a better
life. He knew the twins would also expect
checks, but this gift was at least a stab at
keeping his privileged grandchildren's feet
on the ground.

The burglary had ruined those plans. And
the twin's sixteenth birthday was just a few
weeks away.

Reading about the auction of the original
Claddagh rings, Dermot immediately decided he had to have at least two of them. It
was meant to be! He couldn't believe his
luck. He would be the proud owner of mas-
terpieces painted by an Irish nun and original Claddagh rings. I'll be the toast of every
Irish gathering from coast to coast, he con-
vinced himself. People will be moved by the

story of my journey back to my homeland to obtain the rings for my grandchildren. I'll be written up in every Irish magazine as a caring, loving family man.

Not so deep down, Dermot Finnegan was very insecure.

Dermot had rushed to call Robert, even though it was the middle of the night, and demanded he come back to work.

"We have a trip to plan!" he had cried.

A browbeaten Robert hastily made his way back to chez Finnegan, then called several of Dermot's friends who were used to Dermot's eccentricities and happy to drop everything for a free trip to Ireland. He then started contacting hotels in Galway. The best places were booked. Dermot knew that Sheila and Brian O'Shea were staying at Hennessy Castle.

"Call Hennessy Castle!" Dermot had instructed.

"Didn't you tell me they just had a fire?" Robert asked.

"Just call them!"

Robert did as he was told.

At 10:00 P.M. the whole group would gather at a private airport outside Phoenix, golf clubs in tow, where they would board Dermot's plane and be off to the west of Ireland.

"Shouldn't I let the O'Sheas know that we're coming?" Robert asked.

"Yes, yes. Right away. Tell them not to leave Ireland with those paintings! I want to see my canvases when I walk through the door of Hennessy Castle. And, Robert, don't forget to bring your camera!"

22

Sheila and Brian were miserable as they waited in the chilly car for Margaret Raftery to reappear. There was no radio, and the heat barely worked. One painting was on the backseat. Six more, and they would be home free.

It seemed like a long way off.

Because it was.

"We can always figure out a way to repay the money," Sheila suggested, breaking the silence. "We can sell the house, and we could always borrow—"

Brain hit the steering wheel with his

palm. "Dermot won't want the money. We never should have told him that the paintings were ready and we were on our way to pick them up."

"But Margaret told us they were ready when we spoke to her on the phone, and they were. Who could imagine that she would toss them in her fireplace like a lunatic? If I run into whoever stole that tablecloth, I'll strangle them, I swear I will! If it weren't for them, we'd be on our way to the airport with the paintings this very minute."

Brian winced. "Why would anyone steal a tablecloth?"

"It's beautiful, and it was made by a ghost. Adds to the intrigue."

"There's got to be more to it." Sighing heavily, Brian said, "I shouldn't have told Dermot a nun did the paintings. There's no way to explain ourselves out of this mess. Everyone's going to know we lied."

The cell phone rang. It was Robert.

"Robert, how are you?" Brian asked, trying to sound cheerful. "It's pretty early in the morning out in Phoenix, isn't it? . . . What? . . . You're coming to Hennessy Castle tomorrow? For five days? You're kidding! . . . Why? . . . Claddagh rings, huh. . . . My cousin has one of those. . . . The paintings? . . . Yeah, Sister has a touch of the flu, but she's putting the finishing touches on them as we speak. . . . I know. . . . I know how Dermot can be. . . . We'll see you tomorrow. Looking forward to it." He hung up.

For a moment he couldn't speak.

Neither could Sheila. What she had just heard sent her into a panic. Her heart was pounding, and she thought she might really faint this time.

"Dermot will be here by late tomorrow afternoon," Brian finally managed to say. "He's coming to Hennessy Castle. He wants to see the paintings as soon as he arrives."

"But . . . but even if we have all the paintings to give him, how can we keep it a secret from Margaret and the manager of Hennessy Castle? You know what a big mouth Dermot is. We told Margaret we'd figure a way to honor May Reilly with the paintings. What are we going to do?"

"First, we have to get the paintings, and then we can figure it out."

"Any bright ideas?"

Brian didn't answer. He looked in the

rearview mirror and spotted Margaret hurrying toward the car. She was wiping her face with a handkerchief. "Here she comes now. With no masterpiece under her arm."

Margaret pulled open the door and plopped herself on the backseat. "Whew! I'm knackered, I am."

"What happened?" Brian asked.

"Rory was so glad to meet me. What a nice fella. So caring. He insisted I get on the treadmill for twenty minutes to get my heart rate up, then he had me go a round with the weight machines."

"He *what*?" Sheila asked.

"Rory told me that if I wanted to get my painting back, I had to start working out. I told him I get plenty of exercise cleaning Hennessy Castle and riding my bike, but he said I needed to do something called strength training—weights and all."

"Well, you have obviously started working out," Brian observed. "So where's the painting?"

"Hanging on the wall of his office. It looks grand. Rory has my decal up there, too. Made me feel good. He said that if I came down to the gym five more times, he'd give me back the painting. By then I might be hooked on exercising. I think I already am. Whew!" She laughed. "Whew!"

"I don't think this car will make it down here five more times!" Brian croaked.

"I'll take the bus. I warned Rory about the bad luck that painting might bring him, but he said my health was more important. And I need to get out more. My son told me I should make new friends. It gets so lonesome up there in the cottage all by myself." She fanned herself with her hand. "I'm sweating." She reached into her pocket, but it was empty. "I just had my handkerchief. I must have dropped it. Let me have a look outside." She tried to open the back door, but it wouldn't budge. With a sense of renewed vigor, she flung her body against it. The door flew open and she fell out, facedown, onto the street.

And started to scream.

"Oh my God!" Sheila cried. She and Brian both hopped out of the car and helped a hysterical Margaret to her feet. Blood was trickling from her nose and mouth.

"I told you I had a dream last night that my tooth fell out!" she said, gasping for breath. Gravel and dirt were stuck to her face. Blood stained her hands. "I think one of my teeth was knocked loose!" She reached up and touched her front tooth. A large piece of it broke off in her hand. "Oh, no!" she screeched. "I'm going to die! I'm going to die!"

"No, you're not going to die!" Sheila insisted as she hurriedly pulled tissues out of her purse. "Give me your tooth, and I'll wrap it up. Hold the rest of the tissues against your gum. We'll get you to a dentist."

"She might not need a dentist—" Brian started to say, but Sheila gave him a withering look.

"I'll get in the backseat with Margaret," Sheila told him firmly, putting her arm around the portly, sobbing woman. "Come on, Margaret, let's get in the car. You'll be fine."

"I'm . . . all . . . bloody!" Margaret protested as she started to ease into the backseat.

Brian glanced over, saw the painting that was just inches from the injured Margaret, and, like a shot, raced around to the other side of the car. He pulled open the other back door and rescued Margaret's artwork before it became flecked with blood.

"So . . . much . . . bad . . . luck!" Margaret

cried through the wadded tissue in her mouth. "I'm going . . . to die."

"No, you're not!" Sheila said. "Do you have a dentist?"

Margaret shook her head. "He . . . passed away . . . a couple . . . years ago."

"There must be someone around here we can go to. Maybe Rory knows of someone. If we call the gym, do you think you'll be able to talk to him?" Sheila asked urgently.

"I . . . guess . . . so."

Sheila dialed the number for the gym and asked for Rory. She then handed the phone to Margaret, whose eyes were bulging out of her head. Margaret pulled the bloody tissue out of her mouth. Her breathing was uneven. "Coach . . . do you . . . know of . . . a dentist around here . . . I could . . . see right away?"

"Now?" Rory asked. "What happened? When you left here a couple of minutes ago, you were in good shape."

"I fell . . . in the street. I'm with some friends. They'll take me to a dentist, but we don't . . . know any . . . around here."

"Oh, Margaret, what a bugger! I'm so sorry," Rory said. "I do know a wonderful fella who will fix you up right away. He and his mother just started coming to the gym. His name is Dr. Daniel Sharkey, and his office is a few blocks away. I'll call ahead and tell them you're on your way."

PAGED

23

"The Fun Run was a good idea," Gerard said as he took the piece of paper from Jack and read the three couples' names. "We have so many events for the hard-core runners in this town, it makes sense to finally have a race that isn't competitive."

Regan smiled. "I think Rory's made it his life's mission to get everyone he meets on the road to exercising."

"He has his work cut out for him then, doesn't he?" Gerard asked with amusement. "I have to give him credit. He's very sincere, and I know how hard he worked getting this race launched. He talked about the Fun Run nonstop for months, all over town, practically shaming people into signing up. Louise and I would have been there, but we were on holiday in Dublin that weekend." Gerard paused, held up the list, and read the names to himself, silently moving his lips.

"They're the only people registered for the race Rory couldn't identify," Jack said. "Except for the one couple who signed up at the last minute and illegibly scribbled their names."

Maybe they're authors, Regan thought with slight amusement, thinking of a couple of her mother's writer friends whose signatures were nothing more than a squiggle. If it weren't for their name splashed across the cover of their books, you'd never guess in a million years what the signature inside stood for.

"Hmmm," Gerard murmured, squinting at the list. "Eamonn and Donna Byrne, Joe and Josie Cullen, Brad and Linda Thompson. None of these people are familiar to me, either, but we'll do some checking. One of the young interns here at the radio station covered the race. He goes to the university and works with us part-time." Gerard pressed a button on his phone. "Would you ask Michael to come to my office?"

"Right away," a young female voice responded.

Regan leaned forward in her chair. "It just seems that if Jane and John Doe had the decal from the race on one of their bags, they must have been in the race. The decals weren't for sale, and Rory says they barely had enough to give to everyone who ran the race."

"And even though they're thieves, the decal is hardly something they would have bothered stealing," Jack added.

"I bet they didn't even realize the decal was on their bag when they checked into Hennessy Castle," Regan said. "If they go to all that trouble to disguise themselves, they certainly wouldn't want to have anything on their property that would in any way identify them."

"It's the little details that often trip up criminals, isn't it?" Gerard asked. "After all their grand planning."

"You're right," Regan answered.

There was a tapping on Gerard's open door. Regan and Jack turned around. A young kid who looked all of nineteen was standing in the doorway. He had curly sandy hair, a quick smile, and a certain eagerness. "Hello," he said. "Gerard, you wanted to see me?"

"Yes, Michael." Gerard introduced Regan and Jack.

Michael's eyes lit up. "I've heard so much about you," he said to Jack. "You, too, Regan."

Jack looked at him quizzically. "You have?"

"Indeed. On Gerard's show last week he was talking on and on about you coming to Ireland for your honeymoon and your job in New York and the crimes you both have solved. Your jobs sound so interesting!"

I'm not crazy, Regan thought. I got one of those feelings this morning that my grandmother always talked about. Gerard is the reason that Jane and John Doe knew we'd be here.

"Keeps us busy," Jack answered, maintaining his composure. It was one of the many reasons Regan loved him. Jack always remained unflappable when he had every right to lose it—like not wanting his honeymoon plans broadcast over the airwaves of Galway.

"Hennessy Castle sounded like a great spot to relax," Michael continued. "Who'd have guessed that thieves would follow you there?"

And that's how they knew exactly where we'd be staying, Regan realized. Gerard wasn't kidding when he said the Irish like to exchange information. The problem is that Gerard does it sitting in front of a microphone. She looked over at him. He didn't even flinch. As a matter of fact, he was smiling.

"Yes, yes," Gerard said. "I got such a response from listeners who heard me talking about your job, Jack. They really—" He paused and looked at the less-than-thrilled expressions on Regan's and Jack's faces. "Ohhhh, goodness, you said you didn't know how the Does knew you were here. You don't think they heard about your plans on my show, do you?" he asked, concern on his face but a touch of excitement in his voice.

Yes, Regan thought. I do.

"Sometimes when I'm here late at night, I feel as if I'm talking to the wall. That's why it's always good to have a guest. People call in, but some nights I think everyone in Galway must be asleep. It's nice to know people are out there listening, but to think your criminals could have tuned in to my show? My word!"

Jack shrugged. "Who knows, Gerard? They could have learned about our plans from a lot of sources, I suppose. But it

seems odd that they would go to all the trouble of coming to Ireland to embarrass me
when the only thing they made off with was
May Reilly's tablecloth."

"Don't let May Reilly hear you say that,"
Gerard joked. He adjusted his glasses. "I
didn't mean to invade your privacy. My show
is like a late-night chat. I talk about all sorts
of things. People call in expressing their
opinions, asking questions . . . As a matter
of fact—"

I can't take it, Regan thought.

"—I'd been talking about my niece's upcoming wedding. Then I happened to mention that you two were coming over, etcetera,
etcetera."

Those darned etceteras, Regan thought.
They'll get you every time.

"A woman called in and said she hoped
you'd be staying in one of the fine hotels in
Galway. I told her you were planning to stay
at Hennessy Castle. I guess I shouldn't have
been so specific."

Guess not, Regan thought.

"When was the show?" Jack asked quickly.

"I know exactly when it was!" Michael volunteered quickly. "It was last Monday night.
My birthday. I went back to my dormitory af-

ter having a couple of pints with my friends to celebrate. It was late, and I flipped on Gerard's show. I never listen to it, you know, uh . . . because . . . because—" he stammered, looking to recover "—because I'm usually studying or asleep."

"Last Monday," Jack repeated. "Eight days ago. Which means that if it was Jane Doe calling to ask where we were staying or even if the Does just heard the program, then they were in Ireland a full week before the burglary. That gives us something to go on. And if they were here for the race last November, maybe this is where they like to spend time."

"Galway is a lovely city," Gerard said, nodding. He reached over toward Michael. "Do you recognize any of these names?

The young lad took the piece of paper and looked at it quickly. "I do!" he said with exuberance.

"Who?"

"Eamonn and Donna Byrne."

"And who might they be?"

"They're the parents of a friend of mine at university. The Byrnes live in Dublin and came to visit my friend for the weekend. Jody never gets out of bed before the crack of noon, so her parents decided to run in the race Sunday morning and meet her for brunch afterwards. I saw them at the race. They walked most of the way."

"You don't know the other couples?" Gerard asked.

"No, I'm afraid I don't."

"Michael, what can you tell us about the Fun Run?" Jack asked. "We have reason to believe that Jane and John Doe might have participated."

"Ah, let's see," Michael said. "Well, you know, it was a different kind of race. A lot of laughs and good fun, actually. One woman ran with her baby pram—"

We heard about that, Regan thought.

"—and groups of friends ran together to raise money for different causes. Some people got their elderly parents out there. One guy who had to be about sixty was walking with his mother. I heard her yell at him to zip up his jacket. It was pretty funny. It turns out he's a dentist in town, and she works in his office." Michael laughed. "A friend of mine went there once and said he'd never go back for fear he'd have to wear dentures before he was twenty. The dentist is a frustrated stand-up comic." He paused. "Nothing really crazy happened the day of the race. The only excitement I recall was when a high school kid threw up at the finish line. He ran as hard as he could instead of pacing himself. That's about it."

"Okay then," Regan said. "I'm sure Jane and John Doe made it a point to blend in with the crowd. They're middle-aged and in good shape. The last thing they want to do is attract attention."

Michael shook his head. "It sounds like blend in they did. I wish I had more to tell you."

"And we wish we had more of a description of them," Regan said. She rolled her eyes. "We just learned from the girl who signed up the last-minute runners that there's a possibility our John Doe has a very strange laugh."

"A friend of mine just broke up with a girl because her laugh is so god-awful," Michael said fervently. "And she's absolutely stunning. She's a fine bit of stuff, I tell you! It's such a pity, but my pal couldn't take it anymore. I told him I'd be willing to put up with it for at least a couple of dates.—"

"Thank you, Michael," Gerard said. "You can go back to work now."

"Cheers," Michael responded as he gave Gerard back the list and walked out the door.

Gerard sighed. "If I caused you this trouble, I'm terribly sorry," he said. "I really mean that. The crime rate in Ireland isn't bad, and I never thought—"

"Don't worry about it, Gerard," Jack said with sincerity. "We have no way of knowing if that's how they found out we'd be here. And if it is and we nab them, then we'll have you to thank for drawing them out of their lair. You don't know how much I want to put those two behind bars. They've stolen from so many good and generous people. Lately they've gotten more daring, and this time they set a fire that could have been deadly."

"I'm going to make sure everyone in Galway is on the lookout for the Does," Gerard promised. "If they're here, I'll make sure they won't rest easy. I'll have them looking over their shoulders every minute." With a determined look on his face and the list of names in his hand, he picked up the phone.

With the help of the staff at the radio station, it took only thirty minutes to determine that Joe and Josie Cullen were schoolteachers who had driven up from the Dingle Peninsula on a whim early Sunday morning to join the race. They took pictures to bring back to their students, anxious to teach them that exercise can be fun and it's never too late to start any new venture.

"And Brad and Linda Thompson," Gerard reported, "bought a home last year in a little village south of Galway. Their number is unlisted. As of yet, we haven't come up with any other information about them."

"It's a good start," Jack said. "We'll take a ride into the village now and look around. Gerard, do you think you could get copies of the pictures those teachers took at the race? If they have e-mail, maybe they can scan the photos and send them to you. It might be helpful."

"I'll get on it right away," Gerard said.

"And, Gerard, do you have a tape of last Monday's show?"

Gerard looked a little embarrassed. "I'll have my assistant get the master from the tape library and make a copy. I promise not to edit the parts where I, uh, talked too much, shall we say."

Regan smiled. "We just want to hear the woman caller's voice, the one who asked about where we were staying, that's all."

As they walked out of his office, Gerard put his arm around Regan. "Try not to be late for Louise's Irish stew," he joked. "We'll have ourselves a good meal. Afterwards we can stop in town for a pint at one of the pubs playing music and then come over here to do the show." He paused, and his tone turned serious. "If the Does are still somewhere around Galway, we'll find them. And we'll make their lives miserable."

He needn't have been concerned on that score. Just outside of town, the Does' lives were getting more miserable by the minute.

24

Knuckles white from gripping the arms of Dr.
Sharkey's dental chair for dear life, Bobby
was planning his revenge on the security
guard who knocked out his teeth after he
and Anna had stolen an antique necklace
from a department store in Nanuet, New
York, last Christmas. They had made it out
the door and into the dark snowy parking lot
before the salesclerk, momentarily distracted, realized one of the estate collection
necklaces she had shown them was gone.
Hearing someone shout "Stop them!" Bobby
and Anna began to run toward the car. Anna
flew into the driver's seat, but a burly guard

caught up to Bobby and grabbed his arm as he was getting in the car. Bobby hit the hulking man in the face with his free fist, and the guard returned the favor with a punch that landed squarely on Bobby's mouth. Enraged, Bobby pushed the guard as hard as he could, which normally wouldn't have been effective, given the guard's size, but the man slipped on the icy pavement and fell. Bobby jumped into the car, Anna floored the gas pedal, and the car screeched out of the parking lot, slipping and sliding.

Stealing that necklace was a stupid, impulsive thing to do. They certainly hadn't planned it. They were shopping for a special present for Anna's mother, who had been complaining that they didn't visit her enough. The salesclerk made it too easy for them to walk off with the sapphire and diamond necklace. Being who they were, they couldn't resist.

And for their trouble, Bobby ended up minus four front teeth. Each of the carefully planned jobs they had pulled off before that provided them with jewelry worth a couple of hundred grand, and not a scratch on them. The Nanuet necklace was valued at $10,000 retail, which, after paying off Dr. Favorman, left enough for an ice cream soda.

Anna's mother lived in upstate New York. They had promised to visit her and stopped at the mall to buy her Christmas present. Explaining to her why they suddenly couldn't make it home for Christmas had been a challenge, but explaining Bobby's missing teeth would have been harder. They decided to head across the country and put as much distance as possible between the scene of the crime and a trip to the dentist. They dropped off their rental car at the after-hours lot in New York City and boarded a bus to Pennsylvania, where they rented a four-door sedan. Christmas dinner was eaten in a truck stop. Bobby dined on soup and apple sauce. They arrived in Los Angeles to find everyone gone for the holidays and spent a week in a hotel waiting for the highly touted Dr. Favorman to return from St. Bart's.

All for a necklace that meant so little to them.

Bobby really wished he could turn the nitrous back on. He was feeling depressed and scared. There was nothing remotely cheery in the harsh little treatment room, nothing at all to lift a patient's spirits—except, of course, the tank of nitrous, that was now off-limits.

"Your dentist has talent," Sharkey allowed. He was bent over a side table, stirring a grayish paste with a steel utensil. Bobby thought he looked like a mad scientist. "Where did you say the man is based?"

I didn't, Bobby thought, but he had to give an answer. "He's in New York."

"'New York, New York, what a wonderful town,'" Sharkey sang. "Mother and Dad and I went there years ago. It was a brilliant trip. Brilliant."

"Um-hmmm," Bobby said.

"If I get back there, I'd love to watch your dentist in action. He's a master." Sharkey straightened up. "I'll fix you up with this temporary cap. It should hold you till you get home. Now open wide . . ."

Bobby closed his eyes while Dr. Sharkey pushed the cap up against his stub, then picked and poked and prodded inside his mouth.

"Voila!" Sharkey finally announced. "Take a look."

With great trepidation Bobby opened his eyes. Dr. Sharkey held up a mirror to his face. Bobby grimaced at his tired reflection, made worse by the harsh florescent light overhead, and then smiled. A big bulky chunk of matter, resembling an oversized and slightly faded kernel of corn, stood in stark contrast to the rest of his Hollywood smile. He had to squelch the impulse to scream, jump out of the chair, and throw Dr. Sharkey against the wall. I look like Goofy, he thought desperately. But he knew he couldn't make a scene. It was too dangerous with Jack Reilly on his tail.

Dr. Sharkey was smiling expectantly. "Now I have to remind you that this is temporary. If you want me to complete the job and make you a permanent cap, I'd be more than happy to. The lab work will take a little time."

"No," Bobby said immediately. "Thank you, but no. We're flying to Los Angeles, and I'll see my dentist—"

"Didn't you say your dentist was in New York?"

"He is," Bobby insisted. "He is. We had plans to go to Los Angeles first." Get me out of here, he thought. He yanked the bib off his chest. "Thank you, Dr. Sharkey."

"Take a sample of this paste," Sharkey instructed. "If it falls out, and I don't think it will, just . . ."

If it falls off, I'll consider myself lucky, Bobby thought desperately.

Sharkey opened the door to the waiting room. "Mother will take care of you."

Anna jumped up from her rickety chair. One look at Bobby's face, and she knew things weren't good.

"He's all set to go," Dr. Sharkey said cordially, walking over to the reception desk.

"They're paying cash," Mother Sharkey announced.

Dr. Sharkey scribbled on a form and handed it to his mother. "We don't accept cash!"

His mother nodded almost imperceptibly, having heard this joke at least a thousand times. "We have an emergency coming in. Don't put away your special paste. It's another broken tooth."

"This is our day for emergencies!"

Anna quickly paid the bill and escorted a strangely silent Bobby out to the car. Before turning on the ignition, Anna turned to him. "Let's see."

With a crazed look in his eye, Bobby lifted his upper lip.

Anna tried to keep a straight face. "It's okay—" she began.

"It's not okay!" Bobby yelled. "It's horrible. I look like Goofy. We've got to get a flight out tonight."

"No!" Anna said. "You'll be fine for the next few days. I have something very exciting to tell you." She started the car. "We have one more job in Ireland that will make us very happy and"—she added with a laugh—"Jack Reilly very unhappy."

"I want to go to Los Angeles," Bobby insisted as they drove down the block.

"No, Bobby. Listen to me for a minute. They recently discovered priceless Claddagh rings . . ."

Inside the dental office, Dr. Sharkey poured himself a cup of tea from the shamrock-covered thermos.

"How's Daddy?" he asked his mother who, surprisingly, was engrossed in a program offering tips on home decorating.

"I checked on him a little while ago. He's fine."

Upstairs in the living room, Seamus Sharkey was sitting near the window, unseen by people in the street. He passed his time reading detective novels and watching the clients who ventured in and out of his son's dental practice. Ever since a walk-in client had bolted without paying six years ago, he made sure to write down the license plate numbers, makes, and models of every patient's car. He also recorded his impressions of the patients themselves.

Too many dishonest folks in this world, he thought. You can never be too careful. During dinner he liked to hear about all the people Danny had treated that day. Danny told such funny stories about them. He couldn't wait to hear about the two who had just left, but he didn't think their story would be funny. It looked as if the guy had started yelling at the woman he was with as soon as they got in the car.

Seamus leaned forward. Another car had pulled into the driveway, and an older woman was being helped out of the backseat. It seemed odd that a casually dressed yet upscale-looking young couple would be driving around in such a beat-up old wreck. Once again Seamus picked up his notebook and pen from the table next to him.

They don't need a security camera with me around, he thought proudly. Danny boy is

so good to us, I wish I could be of more help
to him. Who knows? he thought. Maybe one
day, even if it's after I've passed, these notes
will be helpful.

25

Keith Waters had been at the office since early morning. He had slept fitfully, aggravated by the fact that Jane and John Doe were ruining Jack's honeymoon. I'm going to do everything I can to track them down, he told himself.

The results of the inquiry into the credit card the couple had used at Hennessy Castle weren't surprising. It was another case of stolen identity. The Does, armed with the social security number of one Earl Norton, had ordered a credit card in Norton's name and had it sent to a P.O. box in Suffern, New York, last month. Suffern was less than an hour's drive from New York City.

So they were in this vicinity not very long ago, Keith thought. But there's no chance they'll darken the doorstep of that post office again. They have probably cut the credit card in half by now. He sighed. Identity theft was becoming an epidemic, making it that much easier for people like the Does to keep on the move.

Keith looked over their file. Besides the event at the Metropolitan Museum of Art that Regan and Jack had attended last year, the Does had also left behind their calling cards after heists in Chicago, Miami, Birmingham, Dallas, Atlanta, London, and Sydney. I guess they're not multilingual, Keith thought. It appears they're only comfortable operating in English-speaking cities. Let's hope for the Parisians' sake that they don't take up French.

Their modus operandi was always the same. They would attend expensive charity galas using false names, pay for the tickets with a fraudulent credit card, and then disappear like Cinderella after they had made their mark. And also like Cinderella, their appearance would change dramatically after the big ball. Jack and his team had worked hard to find a link between the stolen credit cards but had no luck. Keith continued to read the file.

The people who ran the events always remembered a lovely couple who melted into the crowd and then never took their places at dinner. The woman was variously described as blond, brunette, redheaded, or white-haired, but always around five feet six inches tall and always fashionably dressed. The man had blond hair, brown hair, or gray hair and was five feet ten. Sometimes they wore glasses, sometimes colored contact lenses. Sometimes, it seemed, they padded themselves to look heavier. They were always unfailingly polite. No one who welcomed them to the exclusive soirees would suspect that the couple gushing about how pleased they were to become active in another charity were a couple of brazen criminals.

Hennessy Castle, though quite unlike the other jobs, was their ninth known hit in seven years. Keith re-read the notes in the file. He and Jack both thought the Does were committing other crimes they were not taking credit for. There were so many cases of lost or stolen jewelry that remained unsolved—

such as the recent theft at the charity gala held the week before Christmas at the Bridges Hotel in New York City. A woman had discovered her priceless diamond and ruby pin was missing when she and her husband were retrieving their coats at the end of the evening.

"I suppose it could have disappeared during the cocktail party. I just don't know," the woman had said, tearfully.

No calling card had been left, but it still may have been the Does' handiwork. If they were in town for the holidays, they might have wanted to pull off a job to get themselves in the Christmas spirit. They might even have been staying at the Bridges. Security was often lax at some of the exclusive galas held at big hotels. If someone hadn't bought a ticket for the event, it would be obvious that person didn't belong there when it came time to be seated for the dinner. But anyone who dressed the part could slip in during the cocktail hour, have a drink and an hors d'oeuvre, and snatch a purse on his way out the door.

One man had made a career out of crashing parties in New York City, had even written a book about it. But he hadn't been a jewel thief.

Keith picked up the phone and called the Suffern post office. The postmaster, who identified himself as George Hiller, told him that the P.O. box in question had been rented out December 23rd.

"December twenty-third?" Keith repeated, remembering that the gala at the Bridges Hotel had been right before Christmas.

"Yes."

"A credit card obtained fraudulently by a couple of jewel thieves was sent to that P.O. box in March," Keith told Hiller.

"Not surprising," Hiller responded.

"No, unfortunately it's not." Keith paused. "You haven't heard about any jewel thefts up your way, have you?"

"Jewel thefts? No, nothing I can think of offhand, except maybe—"

"Except what?" Keith asked.

"Some jewelry shoplifted from a store near here at Christmas time. But a lot of shoplifting occurs over the holidays."

"I'd like to hear about it anyway," Keith said matter-of-factly.

"Okay," Hiller said. "I'm just thinking back. . . . This box was rented on the twenty-third of December. . . . Wait a minute. The theft happened on that very day! We had a little Christmas party here at the post office after work. Then I drove over to the Nanuet mall to do Christmas shopping. My wife buys most of our gifts, or I should say all, except for what I buy her, and I always wait until the last minute. Every year I say I'm going to change, but I never do. Anyway, among other things I wanted to see if I could find a nice pair of earrings for her at Bam's, a big department store at the mall. When I got there, the place was a madhouse with people like me running around. And some of the salesclerks at the jewelry counter were upset. Everyone was buzzing about a couple who had sauntered out of the store with an expensive necklace. The security guard almost caught them, but they got away."

"Stores lose a lot of revenue around the holidays from shoplifting," Keith said. "They do the best they can to discourage it, but it's going to happen."

"I know, but this necklace was worth ten thousand dollars."

Ten thousand dollars sounded too minor league for people like the Does, Keith thought. But the theft had occurred on the very day they rented a P.O. box in a town nearby. "You say the store is called Bam's?" he asked.

"Yes, Bam's. December twenty-third. Definitely." Hiller chuckled. "When I got home with the packages, my wife was relaxing by the fire, sipping eggnog and watching television. I was wet and cold, and started complaining about the long lines at the stores. She teased me and asked what the big rush was, that I had another entire shopping day before Christmas."

"That's when I get my shopping done," Keith joked. "Listen, thanks so much." A few minutes later he had Denny Corra, the head of security at Bam's, on the line.

"A middle-aged couple stole the necklace," Corra informed him. "I'll be happy to get out the security tapes. There was nothing special about them. The saleswoman who showed them the necklace was very upset and said she'd understand if the store wanted to fire her. But management insisted she stay. She's good at what she does. That day she'd been working twelve hours and was caught off guard."

"When is she working again?" Keith asked. "I'd like to speak to her."

"Let me check. I'll call you back in a few minutes."

Keith hung up and sat at his desk, deep in thought. Could the Does have bothered with such a small job? When the phone on his desk rang a few minutes later, he quickly grabbed it.

"She's working from four until ten tonight," Corra reported. "You can talk to her in my office and go over the tapes. I know she'd love to help in any way she can. Nothing would thrill her more than if those two were locked up."

And nothing would thrill us more, Keith thought, than if those two were caught *and* turned out to be Jane and John Doe.

26

Regan and Jack returned to their rental car on the street outside Gerard's office.

"I love you, Jack," Regan said.

Jack smiled. As he was starting the car, he leaned over for a kiss from his bride. "Are you telling me that at this particular moment because—"

"You know exactly why I'm telling you right now. My mother always told me to find someone with a good disposition who will let things roll off his back."

Jack's eyes twinkled. "Regan, don't you think it occurred to me that Gerard might have mentioned our plans to visit Ireland on the air? He's a radio show host with a lot of time to fill every night."

"You thought he might have talked about us on the air?" Regan asked incredulously. "I wish you'd said something."

"Why? You didn't." Jack pulled out of their parking space, chuckling, obviously very pleased with himself.

Regan felt a moment of delirious happiness. She remembered what she had told Kit not long after meeting Jack: "He gets me, Kit."

It was what they both had been looking for—that indefinable bond between two people that had nothing to do with shared interests, compatability ratings, and goals for retirement. Regan smiled to herself. She could just imagine bringing home the very wrong guy to Nora and Luke, someone who had no outwardly redeeming values, and telling them, "But he gets me."

"Jack, can you imagine what Jane and John Doe would think if they found out we were tracking them down based on a decal from a road race?" Regan asked.

"Let's hope exercise proves to be their undoing."

One of Gerard's coworkers had given them general directions to Westweg, the town where Brad and Linda Thompson had recently purchased a home. "It's a little village," he'd said. "You'd best stop in town and ask for specific directions. It gets very tricky down there. Some of the houses and cottages can be impossible to find if you don't know the area."

"Sounds like a place they'd want to live," Jack had commented.

After an hour of driving on endless scenic country roads and passing far more cows than people, they found themselves on the tiny main street of Westweg.

"Slow down!" Regan cautioned. "We almost missed the whole town."

Jack pulled over and turned off the ignition. It was completely quiet, except for the sound of a slight breeze blowing through the trees. Not a soul was in sight. "Okay," Jack said, looking around. "We have our choice of the pub, the chemist, the butcher, or the general store."

"The store has two tables by the window. Maybe we can get a cup of tea and a bit of gossip."

"Let's hope we'll find someone who likes to share information as much as Gerard," Jack said as he got out of the car.

Inside the small store, all the shelves were crammed with food and supplies. It seemed to have all the basics for survival, but if you wanted eighteen cereals to choose from, a trip to Galway would be in order.

A sturdy, round-faced woman with wavy auburn hair, pulled back in a ponytail that was losing its grip, greeted them warmly. She was wearing an apron over a fisherman's sweater and jeans. "May I help you?" she asked, wiping her hands on her apron. "My husband and I were in the back unpacking boxes."

"We were wondering if we could get a cup of tea," Regan inquired.

"Of course. Have a seat. Anything to eat? A sandwich perhaps?"

Regan and Jack looked at each other. They were both hungry and wouldn't have dinner for several more hours. Jack nodded. "Sure."

"Ham and cheese on homemade bread?"

"That sounds wonderful," Regan said.

Jack and Regan sat at one of the tables. In no time the fortyish woman was hurrying from the back of the store, carrying sandwiches and a pot of tea. "You're passing through here, are you?" she asked, plunking the plates down on the small table.

"We're actually looking to speak to a couple of people who live in town," Jack answered in a neutral tone.

"And who would that be?"

"Brad and Linda Thompson."

"Oh, yes, yes, yes," the woman said.

"Do you know them?" Regan asked.

The woman took the question as an invitation to join them. She slumped into a chair at the next table which was just a few feet away. "I'll sit and talk to you for a minute. I'm tired of unpacking boxes. My name is Breda."

Regan and Jack introduced themselves. "So you know the Thompsons?" Regan asked again.

"Well, I can't say I exactly know them. I know them, but I don't know them." Breda laughed. "That's the way it is with a lot of people around here. At first they seem really friendly, but the heart of the matter is, they keep their distance." She nodded knowingly. "My husband tells me I talk too much and ask too many questions." She paused. "Why do you want to speak to the Thompsons?"

"We want to find out if they remember anything about a couple they might have encountered in a road race last November," Jack told her, omitting the fact that the Thompsons were people they wanted to check out. "You see, we are staying at Hennessy Castle and . . ." He explained about the jewel thieves and the stolen tablecloth and that they had reason to believe Jane and John Doe had run in the Fun Run in Galway.

Breda's mouth dropped. "I heard on the radio about the thieves who were out to get you, but I didn't know they might have been in the Fun Run last November! Let me get myself a cup of tea." She got up and hurried to the back.

"Perfect," Regan said to Jack. Jack winked at her as she bit into her sandwich. It was delicious.

"Here I come," Breda bellowed a moment later. She appeared again, plopping back down in her chair. "So you think these thieves might be staying in Ireland?"

"We don't know," Jack answered honestly. "But they were certainly at Hennessy Castle, and they have to go somewhere when they're not working."

"And Brad and Linda ran in the Fun Run?"

"We think so." Jack asked casually, "What can you tell us about Brad and Linda?"

Breda's eyes glittered with excitement as she pursed her lips. "They're Americans."

So far, so good, Regan thought.

"They're new around here. I haven't seen them much. They don't live here all the time."

Description still fits, Regan mused.

"What do they do?" Jack asked.

"I couldn't tell you. They're middle-aged; maybe they're retired. They've been in the store a handful of times and said something about buying their house as an investment. They're always pleasant but don't volunteer much. I've never seen them at church or at anything in town here. Not that there's much to do."

"You don't have a phone number for them, do you?" Jack asked.

"No."

Regan was dying to ask Breda what the Thompsons looked like, but it would sound too suspicious. "We have the Thompsons' address," Regan said, "but we didn't want to just show up and ring their bell."

"I understand," Breda said. "People buy houses around here because they want their privacy. Some people come here to write or paint in peace. Others are looking for the answer to the question, 'What's it all about, Alfie?' and think they'll find it in the middle of a bog. I don't know. But the Thompsons seem like decent people who would want to help you catch a couple of criminals. You say they're jewel thieves, right? Let me tell you something, Linda Thompson has deadly jewelry! You don't see many people wearing the baubles she does to come in and buy a bag of feed. I'm sure Linda Thompson would be happy to answer your questions." Breda jumped up. "Let's see if they're home. I'll drive you down there right now. We received some wonderful jam in today's delivery that the Thompsons specifically told me they liked. It'll be a friendly gesture to drop off a jar, say hello, and introduce you."

"You've been to their house before?" Regan asked.

"Not inside, but I know where everyone in these parts lives. I drove by the Thompsons' cottage after they moved in."

"What about the store?" Regan asked, looking around.

"Does it look busy to you? I think my husband can handle it by himself until I get back." She took off her apron and yelled, "Sam! I'll be back in a while!"

"Okay" came the response.

"Let's go," Breda commanded, grabbing her car keys from a hook by the door.

They were actually the keys to her little pickup truck.

Regan sat in the middle between Jack and Breda, who apparently thought she was driving an ambulance. They barreled down the tiny main street of Westweg.

"I love to be out in the wide-open spaces," Breda said with exuberance. "I live in the country, but I'm cooped up in that store for hours on end. It's not bad but . . ." She pressed her foot on the accelerator and zoomed around a slow-moving truck that was weighted down with piles of sod.

Regan felt her life passing before her eyes. We should have offered to follow her, she thought.

Jack cleared his throat. "Have you lived here long?"

"I lived in the next village growing up. I met Sam when we were both twenty. We're married twenty-five years. Two kids. Whoops!" She turned the truck quickly onto a road full of potholes. "Sorry. I'm on auto-pilot, thinking

I was on my way home. I'd better slow down with all these bumps."

There is a God, Regan thought.

After ten more minutes of bumping along, they made a turn and drove through a set of gates toward a cottage in the distance where a man and a woman were outside gardening. "They're here!" Breda exulted as she started honking the horn and waving. "I wonder why they haven't been in the store!"

This isn't how I imagined we'd approach people who might be Jane and John Doe, Regan thought, her heart beating fast. She could tell that Jack was also a little tense. They had programmed a main number of the garda into Jack's cell phone and promised to contact the officials if they had anything to report about the Does or if they needed help.

The Thompsons glanced over at the oncoming truck and started to get up from the ground as Breda pulled closer and closer. But when the smiling couple straightened up to their full size, Regan's heightened emotions fell flat.

The woman was head and shoulders taller than the man.

Clearly they were not Jane and John Doe.

Jack turned to look at Regan. She could tell he was disappointed. "Come on," he said, squeezing her hand. "Let's see what they have to tell us about the Fun Run."

27

Dr. Sharkey fixed up Margaret Raftery with a temporary cap nearly identical to Bobby's. "We're lucky your whole tooth didn't break off," he told her. "It's going to take a few more visits before we get you in order."

Margaret was floating in the chair, the nitrous oxide mask covering her nose. "It's all right," she said. "I'll kill two birds with one stone and go to the gym when I come back to Galway."

"Isn't Rory wonderful?" Dr. Sharkey asked.

"So he is," Margaret said. "I love him. I just love him. He thinks I'm a wonderful painter."

"You paint?"

"Indeed. And I drew the decal for the Fun Run."

"My mother and I were in the Fun Run!"

"Bully for you."

Sharkey laughed. "That decal was perfect for the race. It captured the spirit of the day. A fun decal for the Fun Run."

"Right. A fun decal for the Fun Run." Margaret started laughing. She hadn't felt this carefree for a long time. She'd completely forgotten that losing her tooth might be a sign of her impending death.

"Who are your friends?" Dr. Sharkey asked, pointing to the receptionist's area.

"They're staying at Hennessy Castle where I work. They ran in the Fun Run, too."

"They did? I must tell Mother. Now take a look, Margaret." He held up the mirror.

Margaret smiled. The ensuing horror she felt penetrated the nitrous oxide haze. "It looks as though it needs a good cleaning, it does.."

"It's a temporary cap," Dr. Sharkey assured her. "The permanent one will be beautiful. Now let me turn on the oxygen and bring you back down to earth."

"With that tooth you'll have to bring me up from hell."

"Breathe in the oxygen," Sharkey said calmly.

"I'll get oxygen outside," Margaret said, pulling off the mask. "I live in the country where there's nothing but fresh air." She swung her legs around and stood. "I don't feel as good as I did five minutes ago."

"You should sit down—"

"No."

"Then go home and get some rest. You'll feel better tomorrow."

Margaret nodded and went out to the waiting room where Brian and Sheila had been sitting in glum silence. "Time to go home," she announced, her face grim with determination. "I want to go straight home this very minute, and I don't want to hear another word about your aunt Eileen. My tooth is throbbing and my head hurts."

Brian and Sheila knew better than to argue. Their art collecting was done for the day.

And they both felt as if they were done for life.

28

Brad and Linda Thompson were also newly-weds and also from New York City, and both had just turned fifty. They had married six months ago, a second marriage for both. Their cottage in Ireland was a vacation retreat where they planned to spend every August. They would rent the cottage in June and July and then visit whenever possible during the rest of the year.

They seem to have a great life, Regan thought as she, Jack, and Breda sat down with the Thompsons in their cheerfully decorated living room. Framed wedding photos filled the shelf above the fireplace. They were an attractive couple. Brad had two grown children from his previous marriage who, judging from the pictures, seemed to approve of their father's new mate.

"We finally got it right," Brad said jovially as he handed glasses of sparkling water to everyone. "Linda and I are having the time of our lives. And we made a pact to always keep in shape, so that's why we did the Fun Run."

"Here I am with a roomful of newlyweds," Breda said, fidgeting with excitement. "I feel like an old married lady."

"Hey," Brad said, "you're doing all right. That husband of yours is a nice guy."

"Indeed!" Breda agreed. "Life gets a little boring at times, but I'm happy."

Regan smiled. Breda was clearly thrilled to have a little excitement thrown into her day, and Linda was obviously a woman in love. She was positively glowing and not just because of her large diamond earrings and numerous gold necklaces, bling not normally found on someone gardening. They must be presents from Brad, Regan decided.

"Ours is a mature love," Linda said, smiling at Brad with adoration and sounding like an earnest talk show guest. "We both found out what we didn't want."

"I found out a few things I didn't want, but there's nothing I can do about it now," Breda said. She laughed, slapped her knee, and looked around the room to make sure everyone appreciated her joke. They did.

Brad worked in finance, and Linda was a real estate agent. They met when he was trying to find an apartment to rent after splitting up with his wife.

"When I met Linda, all the clouds parted," Brad said, gesturing out the front window. "She lit up my life," he declared, sitting on the ottoman in front of Linda's chair and putting his hand on her leg. "I bring her coffee in bed every morning—"

Breda looked awestruck.

"—and never once has she nagged me to take out the garbage."

Just wait, Regan thought.

Jack cleared his throat. Regan could tell he wanted to get down to brass tacks. But Brad wasn't finished.

"Our friends tease us," Brad continued, "because we're so over the moon in love."

Linda giggled, placed her hands on her husband's back, and started to massage his shoulders.

We had better make this fast, Regan

thought. Breda was about to fall off her chair.

"Isn't being a newlywed just wonderful, Regan?" Linda cooed, wrapping her arms around her husband and resting her head on his shoulder.

"Yes," Regan agreed. "We're very happy. But we don't want to keep you, so if you don't mind, we'll just ask a couple of questions about the race and be on our way."

"Do you want to stay for dinner?" Brad asked with great enthusiasm. "We have steaks in the freezer."

"No, thank you," Jack answered. "We're having dinner with a cousin of Regan's in Galway. Gerard Reilly. He has a radio show here."

Linda and Brad's faces were blank. "I've never heard of Gerard Reilly. Have you, honey?" Linda asked, nuzzling her nose against her husband's sweater.

"No."

"Well, anyway, he's expecting us," Jack then quickly gave more details to the Thompsons about why they were there. "We know you signed up for the Fun Run right before the race began. Did you happen to see the very last couple who signed up?

They were probably in their forties. Apparently the woman tripped right near the registration table—and the man had a strange laugh."

Linda lifted her head from Brad's shoulder. "I remember them!"

"You do?" Regan asked.

"Yes! His laugh *was* strange. And there was something about the woman that reminded me of someone I knew, but I couldn't figure out who."

"Someone you knew?" Regan asked.

"Yes. Someone from my past, but I can't place her. I almost went over to talk to her, but she didn't look very approachable. I think she was annoyed that her husband was laughing so hard. Then the race was about to start, and they hurried off. I've met so many people showing apartments, I figured she reminded me of one of the clients I showed a million apartments to who never bought anything. Those people I try to forget."

"What about this woman triggered the memory of someone else?" Regan asked.

"It was after she fell. When she stood up, it was the way she stretched her arms and ran in place for a second."

"A lot of runners do that, honey," Brad said.

"But this was different. And there was something else she did. I just can't think of what it was."

"Did she *look* like someone you knew?" Regan asked.

Linda shook her head. "She had on a cap and big sunglasses and a bulky wind-breaker. I didn't get a good look at her face. It was more of a profile. Oh! That was the other thing. The way her jaw was moving. It looked like she was chewing on a lozenge or something."

This is getting us nowhere, Regan thought. "Was there anything else about her that you remember?" she asked.

"Not really."

"Did either of you notice anything unusual that happened at the race?"

They both shook their heads. "You know how it is in the early stages of love," Brad said, "you only have eyes for each other. You don't notice anything else because you're the only two people in the whole wide world."

"Of course," Jack said, putting down his glass of water on a coaster. "We really appreciate your time. If you think of anything else or figure out who this woman reminded

you of, please contact us." He reached in his
wallet for his card.

Linda grimaced. "I wish I could remember
who it was."

Brad patted her leg. "You will, honey."

They all stood. Regan walked over to take
a closer look at the wedding pictures. "You
were a beautiful bride," she said to Linda
honestly.

Linda smiled. "Thank you."

"She looked gorgeous!" Brad boasted.

"It helped to have a good makeup artist,"
Linda joked. "The one I had at my first wedding eight years ago was absolutely terrific,
but she left town—" Linda put her hand to her
mouth, a shocked expression on her face.

"What is it, baby?" Brad asked.

"That's who that woman reminded me of!
Anna! She did the makeup at my first wedding."

Brad covered his ears. "I can't stand to
hear about your marriage to that awful man,"
he said playfully.

"If we could just talk about the makeup
artist for a minute," Jack said, urgency in his
tone. "You say you lost touch with her?"

"Yes. After my wedding, she did my

makeup a few more times and then one day when I called, her cell phone had been disconnected. No one knew where she was."

"Why did the woman at the race remind you of her?" Regan asked.

"When Anna did the makeup for me and my bridesmaids the day of the wedding, she had to keep bending over because we didn't have a chair that was the right height. Her back started to bother her. She started joking around and did a few stretches and some running in place. That woman at the race was moving and stretching just the way Anna did! She massaged her neck with both hands, exactly as Anna did. And her jaw was moving constantly, just like Anna's! Anna popped breath mints every two seconds. I think she gave some of her clients a complex. You know how when people offer you a breath mint, you think it's because you need it."

"Do you remember her last name?" Regan asked quickly.

"Ohhhh, what was it?" Linda shook her head. "I don't remember. I'll have to call my hairdresser. He recommended her to me. It was eight years ago."

"Can you call your hairdresser now?" Regan asked.

"Sure."

"Here, use my cell phone," Jack said, pulling it out of his pocket. "I'll dial the number for you."

"I know that number by heart," Linda said. "It's a good thing I didn't switch hairdressers, or he'd never take my call. And not many women in New York keep the same hairdresser forever. The number is 212 . . ."

Jack dialed and handed her the phone.

When the receptionist at the salon answered, she told Linda that Rocco was with a very important client and would have to call back.

"Tell Rocco this is urgent!" Linda demanded, authority in her voice. "Tell him I'm calling from my home in Ireland."

"Just a moment."

Regan, Jack, Breda, Brad, and Linda were all standing in the living room, anxiously waiting for Rocco to put down his scissors and come to the phone. Breda had all her fingers crossed.

"Hello, Rocco," Linda said.

They listened as she asked him about Anna.

"I know she disappeared off the face of the earth without saying goodbye. . . . I don't know if she ever got married. . . . What was her last name? . . . Hager . . . that's right. It was Hager. Thanks, Rocco, I'll see you the minute I get back—cut and color. Bye." Linda handed the phone back to Jack. "Anna Hager was a makeup artist in New York City. Rocco recommended her to all his clients for years, then eight years ago she was gone."

"Could something have happened to her?" Regan asked.

Linda shook her head. "When we couldn't find Anna, Rocco went to her apartment to see if she was okay. She'd given her landlord three days' notice, paid the rent, and moved out. It really hurt Rocco's feelings that she didn't tell him. He sent her a lot of clients."

"Thank you, Linda," Regan said. "We'll look into it. It could be that Anna just wanted to make a change in her life."

"New York can be a rat race," Linda said. "And she seemed like such a nice girl. I cannot believe she might be a jewel thief."

"A jewel thief who knows a lot about how to disguise herself," Jack said. "And Anna was a makeup artist. But, listen, we can't convict her yet. We'll follow up on this and let you know what we find."

Linda's face went pale. "I just remembered something Anna told me."

"What?" Regan asked.

"She told me she'd done makeup for a magician who taught her a few tricks . . . like how to steal someone's watch right off their wrist. We laughed about it. It seemed like a joke at the time."

"If Anna is our Jane Doe, then it's not a joke anymore," Jack said. "We'd better get going."

29

Anna and Bobby were almost home. Bobby
had complained about his tooth repeatedly,
questioned the wisdom of stealing the
Claddagh rings, and then to Anna's delight
had lowered his seat and fallen asleep. They
were both exhausted. She longed for some
music but didn't turn on the radio for fear
she'd waken him. We'll go home and take it
easy, she thought, then wondered what they
should have for dinner. Nothing too chewy.

As they entered the village of Westweg,
which was only a fifteen-minute drive from
their home, Anna decided to make a quick
stop. She'd been in the general store once

and remembered they had delicious soup and sandwiches. I'll run in and see what kind of soup they have today, she thought. That's all Bobby will want tonight, I'm sure.

When she parked the car, Bobby didn't even wake up. She quietly got out, crossed the street, and hurried inside the store. The aroma of fresh baked bread and spices filled the shop, and she was glad she'd made the effort to stop. A man's voice called out from the back. "I'll be right with you. Sorry, my wife ran out for a few minutes. She should be returning soon, at least I hope she will."

"Okay," Anna said politely, looking around. She took a basket and started filling it with groceries. She reached up to a shelf against the wall and grabbed a box of cookies.

"May I help you?"

"Oh!" Anna squeaked, whirling around and taking in the sight of a ruddy-faced, barrel-chested man with black hair and a mustache. "I didn't hear you."

"Are you all right?" he asked, then smiled. "I'm not that scary, am I?"

"No, you're not. I'm very tired, that's all. What's your soup today?"

"Chicken noodle."

"Could I have a large container please?"

"Sure." He turned and headed for the kitchen.

Anna finished shopping, walked to the back, and started unloading her groceries from the basket onto the counter.

"I can't believe my wife isn't back yet," the storekeeper said, putting the hot container on the counter and then ringing up the charges.

"I'm sure she'll show up soon," Anna said.

"You don't know my wife," he grumbled good-naturedly.

Anna paid him in cash and watched as he bagged her items.

"Here you go," he said, pushing the bag toward her. "Well, what do you know, there's my wife now—blathering on in the street. I told her she talks too much."

Anna turned to look. Through the glass window she could see a woman talking ani-matedly to a young couple. Anna gasped. It was Jack Reilly and his wife, Regan!

"What's the matter?" the storekeeper asked. "You seem a little jumpy."

"As I said, I'm tired. It's been a long day. You know what? I'd love to have another large container of soup. It smells delicious. With this damp weather, I'm sure we'll be eating it for days. And my husband doesn't feel well."

"That's a shame. But nothing tastes better than a nice bowl of hot chicken soup . . ." He turned toward the stove, his sentence trailing off.

Anna stood with her back to the window. She was frantic. Jack Reilly probably doesn't know what we look like, but the last thing I want to do is come face-to-face with him. I just hope Bobby doesn't wake up. If he does and decides to get out of the car without realizing Jack Reilly's in the street. . . . I should never have stopped here—never. Nervously, Anna reached in her purse, retrieved a breath mint, and popped it in her mouth. As she bit into it, she could hear the door to the store creaking open. Anna held her breath.

"Let me know what happens, would you, please?" a woman's voice yelled, obviously talking to someone outside. "And if you need my help at all, please, just give a call. . . . Grand, that would be grand. . . . Brilliant . . ."

"Here's your soup. I hope your husband feels better."

"Thank you." Anna paid again and slowly put the change in her purse.

The sound of the door closing and a

woman calling "I'm back!" was music to Anna's ears. She turned to catch a glimpse of Jack Reilly and his wife getting into a car and driving off. Flooded with relief, Anna picked up her bag of groceries and headed for the door.

"Get everything you need?" the woman asked her.

"Yes, thank you." Anna hurried outside and across the small street to the safety of her car. Though thrilled to have made her escape, she would have been very interested in what the woman inside the store was telling her husband. Breda couldn't get the words out fast enough.

"And, Sam, they think Jane Doe's real name might be Anna!"

30

There wasn't much conversation on the ride back to Margaret's cottage. The car sputtered along, sounding as if it might give up the ghost at any moment, and Margaret made noises that indicated she was experiencing dental discomfort.

When they finally turned onto Margaret's property, there was a collective sigh of relief. Brian pulled the car around to the back of the house, where the sight of a little greenhouse out in the field was too much for him to bear. Margaret had informed them that after her husband died she had transformed the greenhouse into a studio where she could paint.

"I threw out all his junk and set up my canvas," she'd explained. "That was my first mistake."

Brian parked and turned off the engine.

"Home sweet home," Margaret muttered. "I can't wait to take to my bed."

"Let us help you get inside," Sheila said, holding Margaret's painting in her lap. Neither Sheila nor Brian was quite sure how they were going to keep it in their possession.

"I don't need any help," Margaret said. She opened the back door of the car and hoisted herself out.

Sheila and Brian looked at each other and followed suit.

"Give me the painting," Margaret said.

Brian walked around the car and put a comforting hand on Margaret's shoulder. "Margaret, I'm worried about you. We'll take care of the painting until we figure out how to properly honor May Reilly. I don't want you to be alone with the painting if there's any chance it'll cause you more bad luck. Are you sure you don't want us to stay with you? We're happy to. We can sleep on the couch and then maybe tomorrow we can get an early start and collect the rest of the paintings from your friends."

Margaret looked at him aghast. "I don't want you staying in my home. No man has ever slept here except my husband and my son. I'm fine here all alone. I've been alone since my husband died. I can take care of myself!" She turned, went into the cottage, and slammed the door.

Sheila and Brian hurried to their car, the painting in Sheila's hands. They wanted to get out of there before Margaret opened the door and started yelling for her artwork.

Margaret was beside herself. The nerve of him, she thought. In the bathroom, she flicked on the light and checked on her tooth in the tiny mirror above the sink. "Disgraceful," she muttered. "I hope I don't die." Without even bothering to make a cup of tea, she lay down on her lumpy bed, fell asleep, and began to dream of May Reilly.

Out on the road, Sheila and Brian realized they couldn't carry the twelve-by-fifteen painting into Hennessy Castle. Until this morning that very painting had been hanging on Neil Buckley's wall. They pulled into a little parking lot near a graveyard and carefully placed it in the trunk of their rental car.

Unbeknownst to them, May Reilly's grave was within spitting distance. A sudden gust of wind blew through the trees, causing them to sway ominously.

"It's getting chilly," Sheila said, rubbing her arms.

Back at Hennessy Castle, a female clerk at the front desk greeted them. "Welcome home!"

"Thank you," Sheila responded.

"We have good news! A small stove was delivered this afternoon, so we'll be able to serve a limited menu in the dining room tonight! Isn't that grand?"

"It's just peachy," Brian muttered under his breath.

"Will we be able to get room service?" Sheila asked.

"Certainly. We'll be happy to accommodate you."

As Sheila and Brian walked through the deserted lounge and down the dimly lit hallway, the castle felt eerily quiet. Gray light filtered through the windows. It seemed as though a pall had fallen over the entire property.

Inside their room, Brian sat on their bed and put his head in his hands.

Sheila took a seat at the dressing table facing him. "What are we going to do?" she asked.

Brian stood, walked over to the desk, and turned on the computer.

"Talk to me," Sheila said.

"I have a plan."

Sheila's eyes brightened. "You do? What is it?"

"Now I played football in college—"

Sheila resisted the impulse to roll her eyes. "Yes, I know."

"We always had to think about what our opponents might do—how they'd react. Put ourselves in their shoes. Take advantage of their weakness."

"Uh-huh."

"Margaret is our opponent."

"Right."

"She bases her decisions on superstitions and fear."

"Right."

"Tonight we're going to scare the wits out of her."

"Brian!" Sheila sounded horrified.

"We have to. But we'll be nice about it. You're going to dress as May Reilly and knock on her window when she's sleeping.

You'll instruct her to get the paintings back from her friends—or else."

"Are you out of your mind?"

"No. It's our only hope. You can't go into battle without a strategy. Now we just have to get the tools to implement our plan." He logged onto the computer and tapped in his password.

Sheila sat there, stunned. "What are the tools?"

"A wig, a cape—you know, the usual things ghosts are known to wear."

"I don't think there's a costume shop in the village," Sheila said sarcastically.

"I'm sure there isn't. Let's just hope there's one in Galway." He tapped on the keys of the computer. "Thank God for these search engines."

"Brian, did you ever think that we might scare that poor woman to death? It's possible, you know."

"It's *your* job to make sure that doesn't happen. Practice being May Reilly—a firm but benevolent ghost." He laughed. "Whhoooooahhhhhhhhh."

Sheila stood and went into the bathroom, shaking her head.

Down the road, in the graveyard, another

strong gust of wind blew around May Reilly's tombstone. Leaves fell from the trees and skittered across the ground. A bolt of lightning followed by a crack of thunder pierced the air, and once again it started to pour.

31

Clara, sitting at the reception desk of the gym, was bored out of her mind. She had done her nails, read a pile of beauty magazines, and stared out the window. One of the magazine articles gave tips on how to look your best all day at work. After all, so many romances bloomed in the workplace. Not in *this* workplace, Clara thought. There's not a prayer Prince Charming will walk through that door.

Her day had been brightened by the Americans asking her questions about the couple at the Fun Run. Clara and Maebeth had been on and off the phone all afternoon, discussing the man with the weird laugh. It wasn't unusual. Anytime a thought passed through Clara's mind that she deemed worthy of a discussion with Maebeth, or vice versa, she picked up the phone. As a result they spoke at least twelve times a day.

Maebeth worked as a waitress from 6:00 P.M. to midnight, which unfortunately meant there wasn't much time for chats in the evenings.

Clara rested her chin on her hand. Was there anything else weird about that couple? she wondered. That laugh was so embarrassing. If my dad laughed like that, I'd die. She was sure that Maebeth would agree. Clara reached for the phone and dialed.

"What's new?" Clara asked when Maebeth answered.

"Nothing. *Henh, henh, henh.*"

Clara giggled with abandon. "Wouldn't you just die if your friends were over your house and your dad started laughing like that?"

"Totally die."

"It would be so exciting if they found those two. Wouldn't that be the best? We could tell everyone we were part of a criminal investigation. I just wish we knew their names."

"I know. All they said was hon . . . sweetie . . . hon. I was like, gag me. And remember when she fell? He was laughing and said, 'Are you okay, hon?' And she was so mad. She's like, 'Yes, sweetie.' It sounded weird, didn't it?"

"I, like, totally forgot about that."

"Hon, sweetie, hon, sweetie. Gross."

"I wonder if I should call that American guy who was here asking about them."

"Why?"

"To tell them they called each other hon and sweetie all the time."

"You think?"

"Maybe."

"I've got to go. My mom's bellowing to me from downstairs."

When Clara hung up the phone, she sat there staring. Why not? she thought. I have nothing better to do. She dug out Jack Reilly's card from her purse and started to dial.

32

On the ride up to Gerard's house, Jack called Keith and told him to find out everything he could about Anna Hager.

"She dropped out of sight about eight years ago," Jack said. "And not long after that, Jane and John Doe fell from the sky."

"I will, boss. And I've got news for you." Keith filled Jack in on the post office box in Suffern, New York, where the credit card used at Hennessy Castle was sent, and the jewelry theft at the Nanuet Mall. "It doesn't sound like their kind of job, but I'm heading up to the Nanuet Mall this afternoon to view the security tapes and talk to the saleswoman who had been showing the couple the necklace."

"Find out if he had a strange laugh and if she was sucking on a breath mint," Jack suggested wryly.

Keith chuckled. "The head of security told me that the saleswoman is really angry, which is good. Something tells me she'll have a lot to say."

It was a quarter to six when Jack and Regan pulled into Gerard's neighborhood. They had just parked in front of Gerard's pleasant-looking house when Jack's cell phone rang. It was Clara, the receptionist at the Get in Shape gym. Jack listened as she told him about the terms of endearment Jane and John Doe used for each other.

"Hon and sweetie?" Jack repeated.

"Yes. I forgot, but my friend Maebeth reminded me."

"Thanks, Clara. We believe her name might be Anna. Does that ring a bell with you?"

"No, but I'll ask Maebeth if it rings her bell."

Jack smiled. "Okay. And thanks again. If you or Maebeth remember anything else, don't hesitate to call."

Jack hung up and put the cell phone in his pocket.

"Hon and sweetie?" Regan asked as they walked up the path to Gerard's front door.

"Our friend Clara says that's what the couple at the race called each other," Jack said with a shrug.

"Occasionally my parents call each other hon and sweetie," Regan said as she rang Gerard's doorbell. She smiled. "Maybe they have a secret criminal life. Or maybe Jane and John Doe are just another loving couple."

"Maybe Jane and John Doe are just smart enough not to address each other by their real names in public."

"Then he should be smart enough to curb his crazy laugh."

"You're right, Regan," Jack said.

The door was pulled open. "Welcome!" Gerard cried. "Come in!"

As Regan stepped into the warmth of Gerard's living room, she immediately felt a sense of belonging, just as she had when she and Kit visited more than ten years earlier. She remembered the cozy rooms filled with family pictures, including one of Regan and Gerard's mutual great-grandparents on their wedding day. Most of the relatives in

the photos were black Irish, like Regan—
dark haired, light skinned, with blue eyes.
This is my clan, Regan thought. We share
bloodlines, and as my mother says, our DNA
is covered with shamrocks. That's why I feel
so comfortable here in Gerard's house.

Louise, a vivacious, pretty woman with
chestnut brown hair and green eyes,
stepped out of the kitchen to greet them.
"Regan!" she said, extending her arms for a
hug. "And Jack! Oh, he's a handsome one,
he is!"

"Regan, I knew I'd like your family," Jack
joked.

They sat in the living room, and over a
glass of wine Jack and Regan explained
what had transpired in Westweg.

"That's wonderful!" Gerard said. "You're on
their tail then."

"We'll see," Jack answered. "Even if the
Does have already left Ireland, it gives us
something to go on. But Gerard," he said,
"that's not something I'll mention on the
show tonight. The fact that Jane and John
Doe left a note for me at the castle has been
made public. They have to know we're looking for them. I don't want to scare them off if
they're still in Ireland."

"Of course not, Jack! We'll say as much as you want about the case and nothing more. You can stay on the air as long as you want. I have one other guest tonight who's a very interesting fellow. As a matter of fact, Regan, your mother called before, and I told her all about him."

"Who's that?"

"An elderly gentleman named Shane Magillicuddy. He recently discovered original Claddagh rings bearing Richard Joyce's stamp hidden behind a brick in the basement of his home."

Jack and Regan listened with great interest about the history of the rings and the upcoming auction.

"No one is sure." Gerard said, "if Joyce designed the original ring himself or if he came across the design in his travels. True romantics believe that he designed the ring when he was enslaved and pining for his sweetheart. The hands of the ring represent friendship, the crown loyalty, and the heart love."

"Did you know that more than two hundred Claddagh rings were discovered in the ruins of the World Trade Center?" Regan asked Gerard.

"I did indeed," Gerard said sadly. "Bless their souls. I read one story about a fireman who was killed that day. He was wearing a Claddagh ring. Now his son wears it."

"I heard that," Jack said quietly.

Gerard put down his glass. "Claddagh rings have such a strong meaning for the Irish. They're passed down from generation to generation. Regan, did you know that our great-grandparents exchanged Claddagh rings at their wedding?"

"They did?" Regan asked.

Gerard went over to a bookshelf and reached for the old black-and-white picture of Hugh and Bridget Reilly that was taken on their wedding day. "You can't tell that the rings they're wearing are Claddaghs," Gerard said, "but they are." He handed the picture to Regan. "People don't really use the Claddagh rings as wedding bands anymore."

Regan and Jack, who were sitting together on the couch, studied the old photograph. Regan smiled. Hugh and Bridget. They were so young, but their expressions were serious. I would love to have known them, she thought. To think that their son, my grandfather Paul, immigrated to America. My life would have been so different if he hadn't.

Actually, Regan corrected herself, if he hadn't immigrated to America, I would never have been born! Her grandparents had met in New York City. Regan looked up at Gerard and pointed to the picture. "What happened to their rings?" she asked.

"After they died, their only daughter, Bridget, inherited them. Bridget, as you know, was your grandfather's sister. Bridget passed them on to her children, Hugh and Bridget, who were here years ago when you visited with your parents, Regan. You probably don't remember. They're both around my age. Hugh lives down in Cork, and Bridget is over in England."

"I'm getting confused," Jack said.

Gerard laughed. "When it comes to following the Reilly clan, that's easy."

"My Reilly relatives live not far from Cork," Jack said. "I was going to call them and maybe take a ride down there, but I don't think that's going to happen on this trip."

"And I was hoping to show you the farm in Roscommon where Hugh and Bridget raised our grandfathers, but that will have to wait as well, I'm afraid."

Regan stared at the rings her great-grandparents were wearing and then looked up at Gerard. "The auction of the rings should be really interesting. To think that they were made over three hundred years ago . . ."

Gerard nodded. "I bet my guest tonight, Mr. Magillicuddy, is going to be surprised at how much they fetch. If he had promoted this auction around the world, Lord knows what response he might have gotten. But as the expression goes, the rings are burning a hole in his pocket. And he hasn't been feeling well. I think he wanted to have the auction before he got too sick or whatever. . . . He joked that he read the obituaries first thing every morning to see if his name was there."

"The Irish sports pages," Jack said.

"Aren't they, though?" Gerard asked. "When I spoke to Magillicuddy on the phone, he was funny and sounded full of life. I think the discovery of the rings has given him a renewed sense of purpose. He's spending all his time trying to figure out where he'll donate the auction proceeds. And, believe me, as we speak every known charity is courting him!"

"Come along!" Louise called to them from the dining room. "And bring your appetites!"

The Irish stew was delicious. Regan and

Jack were tired, but the hearty meal gave them the boost they needed to keep going. Gerard's show didn't start until 10:00 P.M. On the way to the radio station they planned to stop with Gerard and Louise at a pub in town to listen to Irish folk music. Then, after the show, Regan and Jack would drive back to Hennessy Castle.

"You both must be exhausted," Louise said as she insisted Regan and Jack stay seated while she cleared the dishes from the table. "I hope you get a good rest tonight. No disturbances such as fire alarms going off at four A.M.!"

And no ghosts out on the lawn, Regan thought. She looked at Jack, who smiled at her knowingly. He was thinking the same thing.

33

Neil Buckley was never so happy to call it a day as when he left Hennessy Castle early Tuesday evening. Things were looking up, with the arrival of a little stove and the impending arrival of the entourage from the United States. But there were only two couples in residence at the castle that night, the Reillys and the O'Sheas.

The O'Sheas had stayed at Hennessy Castle twice before and seemed like a nice young couple. But why, Neil wondered, did Jack Reilly have to spend his honeymoon under my watch? Just my luck that two criminals who were out to get him followed him to the castle. Maybe it's the curse of the Reillys. And with May Reilly's tablecloth missing from the memorabilia room, the story about her ghost haunting the castle would lose some of its intrigue. That tablecloth had been part of Hennessy Castle's lore. Neil suddenly had the thought that they should have left the memorabilia room as a crime scene, but then dismissed it. A guest might have cut himself on one of the pieces of broken glass.

Oh, well, with any luck we'll get the tablecloth back, he thought as he drove toward his home near Galway. And we'll get lots of good publicity. When he had taken the job as manager of Hennessy Castle several years ago, he was told to shake things up.

"There are a lot of castles and old stately hotels in Ireland for tourists to choose from," he was told. "We have to make Hennessy Castle the number one destination!"

Neil had done his best. Among other things he had worked hard at hiring a top-notch staff, enhanced Hennessy Castle's Website with testimonials from guests who claimed to have seen May Reilly's ghost, and even sent thank-you notes, holiday cards, and birthday cards to everyone who had spent the night at the castle. He had done this from the day he started working there. I've given it my all, he thought. I couldn't predict that criminals would be checking in disguised as old folks.

When he arrived home, Neil's wife, Felicity, greeted him at the door and excitedly pointed to the empty spot on the living room wall where Margaret's painting had hung.

"Darling," Felicity said, her eyes dancing, "Margaret is terrified of May Reilly."

"So am I," he responded as he took off his coat. Felicity was a pistol, always had been. It was certainly true that opposites attract, but sometimes he wished she were a little less gregarious. He was quiet and methodical; she was the life of the party. Their marriage had stood the test of time—forty-one years and counting.

"Can you imagine Margaret thinking that May Reilly is going to haunt her because of the lace in her paintings?" Felicity bubbled, anxious to gossip.

Neil headed toward the kitchen. "I've never met a woman who was as superstitious as Margaret Raftery, except maybe my mother." He opened the refrigerator and grabbed a beer.

"Your mother!" Felicity laughed as she went over to the stove, lifted a lid on a big pot, and stirred a mélange of vegetables energetically. "She thought it was bad luck to cut her fingernails on Sunday! And what day of the week did she say was always a bad day for your family?"

"Tuesday," Neil said. "Today is Tuesday. She wasn't wrong about everything you know," he said defensively.

"Of course not," Felicity acquiesced. "It just made life difficult when she thought so many things we did would 'tempt the fates.' We couldn't even admire our beautiful children because she said it would bring bad luck. And she wanted us to keep the kids barefoot—even in winter!—so the fairies wouldn't kidnap them."

Neil rubbed his eyes. "I know."

"And remember she didn't want us to get married on a Saturday? That was supposed to bring bad luck, too. And she wouldn't come into our first little house until we'd hung a horseshoe *face-up* over the door. Face-up so the good luck wouldn't run out. And, of course, she was always throwing salt over her shoulder whenever anyone dropped anything in the kitchen. My floor always looked as if we were preparing for a snowstorm. I could go on and on."

You already have, Neil thought wearily but muttered an *um-hmmm* in agreement. He sat on a stool at the kitchen counter and gratefully took his first sip of beer. "Poor Margaret," he said, putting down his drink. "She's a bit daft, but she's been such a loyal employee all these years. The theft of the tablecloth has really thrown her off whatever little balance she had." He pondered the events of the day as he watched Felicity, armed with a giant fork, poke at the potatoes in the oven. She'd never been a great cook.

"These need another another ten, maybe fifteen minutes," Felicity mumbled.

"I can't imagine who would have been driving Margaret around today," Neil remarked. "I always had the impression she was a loner."

Felicity shut the oven door and shook her head. "I am so mad at myself! I should have offered to walk her to the car."

"Ah, well," Neil said. "I hope she's planning on coming to work in the morning. We have a group of Americans coming in." He paused. "No matter what, I'm going to make sure everything runs smoothly tomorrow at Hennessy Castle."

Neil should have learned from his mother that it was bad luck to "tempt the fates."

34

When Mother Sharkey and her son closed up shop, they went upstairs where Seamus was making preparations for their evening meal.

Tonight they were having spaghetti, a family favorite.

"I put the water on to boil," Seamus said proudly, "and I set the table. How were things down at the smile center this afternoon?"

"Busy, Daddy," Dr. Sharkey answered. "Two emergencies."

"I can't wait to hear all about them."

"You will. First, I want to get out of these clothes and put on a pair of sweats." He disappeared down the hall, whistling a happy tune.

"Danny's such a good boy," Seamus commented to his wife, Kathleen.

"I'm worried about what's going to happen to him when we're gone," Kathleen responded. "He's going to miss us so much. If only we could find him a nice girl."

Seamus nodded. "It was such a shame he drilled the teeth of that lovely lass he was going around with a few years ago. Things were never the same after that. I thought they were truly in love."

Kathleen pointed her finger at her husband. "The saying goes, 'You shouldn't mix business with pleasure,' but it was on a Sunday, remember? She had a terrible toothache and asked him for help. It wasn't Danny's fault she ended up with an infection and had to have the tooth pulled. Now let's get this food on the table."

Seamus sighed. "Maybe we should have been more encouraging when he wanted to go into show business."

Kathleen waved her hand disgustedly. "And I should have made a living doing the Irish jig."

Seamus knew the discussion was over.

During dinner Seamus asked his son about the emergencies he had handled that afternoon.

"The first," Danny said as he twirled spaghetti onto his fork, "was an American whose cap fell out when he bit into a blueberry pancake that contained a pebble."

"Ouch!" the older Sharkey cried. "I get a pain just thinking about it. Did he have brown hair? And was he with a brown-haired woman?"

"Yes."

"I knew it!"

"Really?"

"Yes. He seemed upset when he got into his car."

"He was laughing when he was in my chair, I can tell you that. The strangest laugh. His wife hurried into the treatment room to see what was going on. She told me he couldn't have any more nitrous oxide."

Mother Sharkey looked up from her spaghetti. "That was when I was upstairs. If I'd been there, I never would have allowed her to interrupt you."

"Thank you, Mother, but it was necessary. She said he had a heart problem."

Kathleen shrugged. "The woman didn't want to fill out the forms. You would have known about his heart problem if she had."

"Fill out the forms?" Danny said with a laugh. "I didn't even get their names."

"You didn't?" Seamus asked, astonishment in his voice. "I'm up here taking notes and writing down license plate numbers in case any of these people turn out to be dishonest, and you didn't even get their names?"

"It's all right, Daddy. They're not coming back. He's going home to his dentist in New York—or Los Angeles. Who knows?"

"What do you mean, son?"

"First he said his dentist was in Los Angeles, then he said New York. It really doesn't matter." Danny opened his mouth and loaded it with spaghetti. "Does it?"

They all ate in silence for several minutes, savoring the delicious spaghetti sauce. It was Seamus's specialty. The bread was crunchy and hot, and the salad tasty.

Finally, Seamus wiped his mouth with his napkin. "You didn't tell me about the other emergency yet."

Danny rolled his eyes. "A woman who works at Hennessy Castle. She fell in the street and knocked out her front tooth. Oh! She's the woman who designed the decal for the Fun Run. Rory at the gym recommended her to me."

"She designed that funny decal?"

"Yes."

"What does she do at Hennessy Castle?"

"She's a housekeeper."

"Based on that decal, I'd say she's a very talented artist. She should pursue her art." Seamus helped himself to another piece of bread. "You know what happened at Hennessy Castle last night, don't you?"

"No," Danny answered.

"I do," Kathleen said. "I saw it on TV today."

"What happened?" Danny asked. "I was so busy every minute, I didn't hear a bit of news."

Seamus explained in great detail. ". . . And this Jack Reilly's wife's cousin is Gerard Reilly, whose radio show I tune into when I can't sleep. Last week I heard him say that his cousin, Regan Reilly, and her husband, Jack, were coming to Ireland for their honeymoon. Jack Reilly is head of the Major Case Squad in New York. I can't wait to hear Gerard's show tonight. I heard a promo for it before. Gerard's going to have Regan and Jack Reilly on as his guests, as well as that lucky so-and-so who discovered the Claddagh rings in his basement."

"He was a lucky so-and-so," Danny agreed.

"Keep the radio low. I need my rest," Kathleen instructed her husband.

"Of course, dear. I just hope I don't fall asleep before Gerard Reilly's show comes on. By ten o'clock I'm usually tuckered out."

"Stay up with me in the living room, and we'll listen together, Daddy."

The older man smiled at his offspring and fondly patted his hand. "I'll make popcorn. Maybe we can call in with questions." He laughed. "It'll be fun. I just hope I don't fall asleep."

Seamus Sharkey wouldn't have slept for days if he had known that not one but two sets of criminals had been under his roof, and he had written them up in his little black book.

35

Sheila and Brian drove back down to Galway, this time in their rental car. They listened to the radio and learned about the note the Does had left for Jack Reilly at Hennessy Castle.

"Oh, God," Sheila said. "Now you know they'll be sticking around. I can't figure out what they were doing at the Get in Shape gym today. It's so odd."

"Let's not worry about it," Brian suggested. "We'll just stick with our plan."

In Galway the O'Sheas bought a black wig, black cape, long black skirt, and old-fashioned white bonnet. They also purchased a black eye pencil to darken Sheila's blond eyebrows, and pure white foundation to make her look as if she'd just risen from the grave. By the time they finished running from one store to another, it was nearly eight o'clock. They carefully loaded all their purchases into the trunk, alongside Margaret's painting, and slammed the trunk shut.

"I feel better already," Brian declared. "We're moving forward."

"I'm glad you feel better," Sheila said, "because I certainly don't. The woman at the wig shop made me very nervous. She asked me *three times* why I was buying a dark wig. You could tell she thought it looked terrible on me."

"It's supposed to look terrible. You're a ghost," Brian said practically. "Listen, the saleswoman probably felt guilty she was selling you something that wasn't the least bit flattering. But, believe me, she was happy to make the sale. Now," he said, looking around the busy street in the heart of Galway, "let's grab a bite to eat."

They found a pub that looked inviting and were seated at a corner banquette. "You picked a good night," the waitress told them. "A couple of our young musicians will start playing in a few minutes. They're really talented. They'll be playing the tin whistle, the flute, the accordion . . ."

"Sounds great, but we can't stay too long," Brian informed her.

"Shame," she said. "What can I get you?"

They ordered pints of Guinness and chicken pot pie. When the waitress walked off, Sheila whispered to Brian, "What time are we going to Margaret's house tonight?"

"Somewhere around midnight."

"Then why can't we stay here too long?"

"I figured we'd go back to the castle and relax. I wouldn't mind taking a shower. I feel a little grubby."

Sheila rolled her eyes. "Don't you think it's a little suspicious if we go back to the castle and then leave again so late? There's not a lot going on in that neck of the woods at midnight."

Brian touched Sheila's nose with his index finger. "You're right, short stuff. That's why we make a good team. I hadn't thought of that."

"Short stuff" is what Brian had called Sheila when they were kids. The childhood nickname still bugged her, but at the moment she chose to ignore it. "It's going to look odd anyway when we show up there at one or two in the morning," she said. "After scaring Margaret Raftery to death," she added.

"Listen, they'll be thrilled to see us, whatever time we get back there. Everyone else was checking out."

"Everyone except Regan and Jack Reilly, I bet. Having them around makes me jumpy," Sheila said.

"Don't worry about it," Brian said. "They're not concerned with us. They're busy looking for two international jewel thieves who stole May Reilly's tablecloth." He laughed. "I'd love to meet those two thieves. They must have some sense of humor to steal a tablecloth."

"Hello!"

Brian and Sheila jerked their heads at the sound of a familiar voice. Regan Reilly was approaching their table! Jack was walking with an older couple toward the back of the pub.

"Hello," Sheila and Brian both managed to say, concealing their sudden angst.

"Fancy meeting you here," Regan said, looking from one to the other.

Sheila managed a laugh. "We didn't think there'd be much food at Hennessy Castle tonight with everything that's happened up there—"

"Oh, I know," Regan said. "You didn't check out either?"

"No, we didn't," Sheila croaked.

"Quick question. Jack and I are investigating the theft of May Reilly's tablecloth. We saw your names on the list of people who ran in the Fun Run last November, here in Galway."

"Great race," Brian interjected.

"Do you remember anything unusual about that day? The couple we're looking for may have run that race."

"No," they answered.

"We just ran the race and went right back to the hotel. It was freezing," Brian explained.

"Well, have a good dinner. I'm sure we'll see you back at the castle. If you think of anything, let me know."

"We will," Sheila said feebly as Regan hurried to join her group.

"This is a first," Brian said. "But I think I just lost my appetite." He was silent for a moment. "You don't think she overheard us, do you?" he asked.

36

"I can't wait to hear Gerard Reilly's show," Anna said anxiously, turning their high-tech stereo to the radio setting.

Bobby barely responded. He was sprawled on the couch where he had parked himself right after they arrived home. Anna had waited on him hand and foot ever since, serving him the chicken soup, cups of tea, crackers, water, cookies, another cup of soup, more crackers. He was milking his dental debacle for everything it was worth. "I'm cold," he whined.

With a glint in her eye, Anna walked over to the chair near the couch, grabbed May

Reilly's priceless tablecloth—which was large enough to cover an extremely long banquet-sized table—and playfully covered him with it.

Like a cranky child, Bobby threw it on the floor. "It's too heavy."

Anna had about as much as she could take. "How about another blueberry pancake before I sit down?" she snapped.

Bobby knew immediately that he had pushed things too far. "I'm sorry," he said contritely, reaching up his arms. "Let's cuddle while we listen to that blabbermouth's show."

Anna took a moment to pout.

"Come on," Bobby pleaded, waving his arms. "Pretty please?"

"Well, all right," she said in a sulking tone. "I'll turn out the lights first so there are no distractions. I want to concentrate on every word Jack Reilly says and every nuance in his voice. He was down in this area for a reason, and I'd love to know what it is—not that he's going to reveal anything." Anna had been a wreck since the Jack Reilly sighting outside the general store. It hadn't bothered Bobby much. But, then again, he had slept through the whole thing.

"There he was . . . in the flesh!" Anna had yelped when she jumped into the car and sped off. "I almost had a conniption."

Anna had flicked on the car radio to hear if there were any updates on the investigation. There were none, but they heard the promo touting Regan and Jack's appearance on Gerard Reilly's show, as well as the man who discovered the Claddagh rings in his basement. In the several hours they were home, it was all Anna could think about. While Bobby fussed and moaned, she watched the clock, waiting for Gerard's show to begin. She hadn't looked forward to a program so much since she was a child counting the hours until the annual showing of *The Wizard of Oz* on television. Finally, there were only five minutes before Gerard's program would start.

"Anna," Bobby said, sounding as sweet as pie, "I just have one more teeny, tiny request before you join me."

"What?" she asked flatly.

"Would you mind getting us a blanket?"

Anna nodded. She picked up May Reilly's tablecloth off the floor, tossed it back on the chair, and hurried toward the bedroom. A moment later she was back with a down comforter. She covered Bobby, who this time was most grateful, turned off the lights, and finally lay down next to him. There they were, in a darkened little cottage on a bleak night in the west of Ireland, spooned together on the couch.

"This is like the olden days," Anna said, "before television was invented. People would gather together around a radio and listen to dramas."

"Do you think I'm stupid?" Bobby asked. "I know all about radio shows. My mother said she had a crush on the Lone Ranger."

The opening music for Gerard's show began to play. It was a jaunty tune about six seconds long. Next, Gerard introduced himself and, as was his custom, began with a joke.

"What's the definition of an Irish gentleman?" Gerard's voice boomed through the speakers. "A man who knows how to play the bagpipes—but doesn't!"

"I like bagpipes," Anna remarked, "except when they get too loud."

"I can't stand them," Bobby declared.

"Good evening ladies, gentlemen, and bagpipe players," Gerard said with a chuckle. "Tonight we have the most interesting guests. One of them I just happen to be related to. . . ."

Anna and Bobby listened with rapt attention as Jack and Regan Reilly related the history of Jane and John Doe, the crime at Hennessy Castle, and the story of May Reilly and her tablecloth.

"Here you are on your honeymoon with my lovely cousin, Regan," Gerard said to Jack, "and these two scallywags are causing trouble for ya."

"They have a personal vendetta against me, that's for sure," Jack answered.

"You can be sure May Reilly will have a personal vendetta against them!" Gerard said. "Legend has it she haunts Hennessy Castle because she was never paid for that tablecloth. Now that it's gone, she'll be even more perturbed. Jane and John Doe had better watch out."

"I'll rip it up and use it as cleaning rags," Anna said spitefully. "Then I'll tell May Reilly to come and get me. I don't believe in ghosts."

"What can our listeners do to help?" Gerard asked. "We don't know if Jane and John Doe are still in Ireland, but let's suppose they are. Is there anything in particular our listeners should be on the lookout for?"

"Unfortunately, they are average-looking people who are very good at disguising themselves," Jack answered.

Anna sighed.

"I think you're beautiful," Bobby whispered in her ear.

"Sssshhhhhhh."

"So there's no scar, no tattoo, nothing to distinguish them physically?" Gerard asked.

"Now there is," Bobby grumbled. "This friggin tooth."

"Not physically, but as I mentioned to you before the show, we—" Jack said.

Anna grabbed Bobby's arm.

"—have reason to believe that the man has a very peculiar laugh."

"What?" Bobby shouted.

"I told you!" Anna said with disgust. "All the work I do on our disguises, and you're going to blow our cover with that stupid laugh of yours."

"It's genetic. It's the way my father laughed."

"Shhhhhh. Let's listen!"

"Yes, you did tell me about the laugh, Jack. And, listeners, we have a young lady on the phone who does an imitation of this strange laugh. She had contact with a couple who Jack Reilly has reason to believe might be Jane and John Doe. For her protection we won't reveal her name. Are you there, honey?"

"Yes. Hello, Gerard. Hello, Jack. Hello, Regan."

They all exchanged greetings.

"Can you laugh the laugh for us?"

"Certainly. *Henh, henh. Henh, henh. Henh, henh, henh.*"

"She's got you down," Anna said.

"My laugh doesn't sound anything like that!" Bobby protested.

"Yes, it does."

Gerard thanked the girl and asked if she'd do the laugh a few more times.

"Henh, henh, henh, henh. Henh, henh, henh. Henh, henh, henh."

"Thanks again, dear," Gerard said. "We really appreciate your help."

Regan and Jack added their thanks.

"Gerard," Regan said, "we want to be clear that the person who laughed like that is not definitively John Doe. But if any of your listeners heard a man laugh like that who possibly fits the description of John Doe, please call the garda. We're in communication with them."

"They can call this radio station as well," Gerard said, reciting the special phone number they had set up for calls. "As I said, we want to do everything we can to help find these two thieves and let you two get back to enjoying your honeymoon trip to Ireland. Regan and Jack, please stay with us while I bring on my next guest, Shane Magillicuddy. . . ."

"Who was that girl?" Anna shrieked. "Where would she have heard you laughing like that?"

"I don't know," Bobby said. "It's hard to make me laugh in the first place. I don't find many things funny."

"You were laughing like a hyena in the dentist's chair today. If Dr. Sharkey is listening, we're in trouble."

"That's why they call nitrous oxide laughing gas. Maybe we should get out of here. Let's leave tomorrow for Los Angeles," Bobby said. "We can forget the Claddagh rings. There will be other jobs."

"Not like this!" Anna protested. "This is a once-in-a-lifetime opportunity. There will always be diamonds and sapphires and rubies and emeralds to steal, but we'll never find jewelry as special as the Claddagh rings. Never again. You can't measure the sentimental appeal of those rings, and they're *old.* I'm telling you, those rings will bring us *tons* of money."

"What about the dentist? You just said he could be trouble."

"We didn't give him our names. It'll be all right. We'll do this job and then leave for Los Angeles."

"Promise?"

"Promise. Now, let's listen to what this guy Magillicuddy has to say."

In the living room of the Sharkey household, the radio was also tuned to the Gerard Reilly show. Seamus was in his favorite chair, his feet propped up on an ottoman. Danny was stretched out on the couch.

They were both snoring.

37

Jack's office, under Keith's direction, was doing everything possible to dig up information about Anna Hager. Keith had called Rocco, Linda Thompson's hairdresser, who told him he had met Anna when they were both hired by a private client. The client wanted to look her best when she faced her husband, who had dumped her for a younger woman, in divorce court.

"We all know that looking fabulous is the best revenge!" Rocco had told Keith. "And Anna was so talented. She could make someone as close to fabulous as humanly possible. How she could transform people with her makeup! She'd work with the face God gave them and bring out their best. I'm not saying she turned all her clients into Ava Gardner, but whew! She was even good futzing with her client's hair if it needed it. Anna had a certain touch. With those hands she performed magic." He laughed. "I guess she still does if she's a jewel thief."

"Innocent until proven guilty," Keith reminded him.

"Sure, whatever. I joked with her that she'd better not start doing hair, or she'd put me out of business."

"Did you spend much time with her?" Keith had asked.

"Not really. We worked together from time to time—fashion shows, weddings, that kind of thing. But we always sent business each other's way, so we talked on the phone quite frequently."

"Was she single?"

"Yes. She'd mentioned a few different boyfriends over the years, but I don't think she was involved with anyone the last time I talked to her."

"Do you know where she grew up?"

"Somewhere in upstate New York. I remember because she talked about her father having to stop at the Baseball Hall of Fame in Cooperstown every summer when they drove to her grandparents' house down south. The whole family was athletic and enjoyed sports, but one trip to that place is enough!"

"They didn't live in Cooperstown?"

"No."

"Were her parents still living in the same town when you knew Anna?"

"Her father had died, but her mother was still in the family home. Anna mentioned a few times that she was going up to her mother's for a visit."

"What about brothers and sisters?"

"Her brother lived out west. I can't remember his name, but I remember Anna saying that he loved to ski. He was a real daredevil, I gather."

It must run in the family, Keith thought. "Was there anything different about Anna's state of mind the last time you two talked?"

"I know she wasn't happy about turning forty. Who is? I mean, please! I thought maybe she went off to find herself by studying with a guru on a mountaintop somewhere and would eventually come to her senses and return to New York. But I never heard from her again. No change of address card, nothing. I must say I was really ticked off."

When Keith hung up, he told the staff to start looking for phone listings of families named Hager in New York State, starting in the area around Cooperstown.

Two hours and many phone calls later, none of the Hagers they'd contacted had been related to Anna. Keith left the office at four o'clock and drove to the Nanuet Mall. He found a parking space near the entrance of Bam's and hurried inside. A security guard escorted him to Denny Corra's office.

Denny, a big, burly man who looked as if he had been hired by Central Casting, rose from his chair. "Keith, I'm pleased to meet you. We'll take this to the conference room next door. The security guard who chased those two bozos to their car and the sales-woman who waited on them are already in there. They're both so anxious to talk to you—they're chomping at the bit! We can look at the tapes in there as well. How about some coffee?"

"I'd love a cup," Keith said.

"How do you take it?"

"Black is fine."

Denny grabbed an Imus mug from a table

behind his desk, poured coffee from the machine that was in constant use in his office, and handed it to Keith. "I don't know what I'd do without coffee."

Keith laughed. "Me, too."

When they stepped into the dingy conference room, the man and woman both stood to greet them. Though they were nothing alike in appearance, they were both quite formidable.

The security guard, a thickly built man who was probably in his early thirties, sported a buzz cut and several tattoos of skulls and crossbones on his muscled arms. The sixtyish woman was tall and commanding, with perfectly coiffed short hair, tasteful gold jewelry, and a stylish business suit. Neither one of them looked like someone you'd want to mess with.

Denny made the introductions, adding, "And Norma and Sonny are two of Bam's best."

Sonny punched his left palm with his right fist. "I should never have let those two get away."

Norma pounded the desk. "I should never have let them walk off with my jewelry!"

These two *are* chomping at the bit, Keith thought.

Together they viewed the grainy security tapes of the couple who had stolen the necklace. It was hard to make out their faces, but on a broad scale they fit the "average" description of Jane and John Doe.

"She had on one of my necklaces," Norma said sternly, "when another customer accidentally knocked a tray of earrings on the floor, scattering jewelry all around my feet. I leaned down to collect the earrings, and when I stood up, those two beasts were gone. It was a nightmare!"

"I ran after them as soon as Norma started shouting," Johnny said with a grimace. "I should have stopped them. I shouldn't have slipped on the ice. I should have gotten their license plate number. But at least I knocked his teeth out"—Sonny held up his hand proudly—"and I have the scars to prove it!"

"You knocked his teeth out?" Keith asked.

Sonny smiled. "At least two of them!"

Keith nodded, turned toward Norma, and asked, "Did they talk about anything in particular?"

"I wrote down everything I could remember after it happened," Norma said. "I don't need my notes anymore because I've gone over them so many times. The man and woman were buying a necklace for her mother. The man joked that he had to buy his mother-in-law something nice because they hadn't visited her enough."

"Did he laugh?" Keith asked.

"No, and I didn't, either. I told him he should *always* buy his mother-in-law something nice and suggested that they buy one of my gorgeous estate necklaces."

"Did they talk about anything else?"

Norma looked embarrassed. "They did say one thing that I wouldn't even mention, but I will because I really want to help you catch them. And then I want a few minutes with them to give them a piece of my mind."

"Me first!" Sonny said, punching his palm.

"What is it you wanted to say?" Keith asked Norma.

"When they first came up to the counter, the woman told me how beautiful my makeup was. She said I applied it like a pro."

38

Regan and Jack stayed on Gerard's program for the first segment of Shane Magillicuddy's interview. Shane was a charming, bearded, quite elderly man whose eyes shone with excitement when he talked about his discovery of the Claddagh rings.

"I plan to keep this one," he told Regan and Jack during a commercial break, pointing to the original Claddagh ring on his finger. "I feel like one of those people who win a huge lottery jackpot in the twilight of their life. I should have cleaned out my basement a long time ago! I could have dined on this story for years! But what the heck, I'm enjoying myself now."

"The ring is simply beautiful," Regan said. "I'm sure your auction will be a big success."

"I hope you'll come as my guests. It'll be a lot of fun."

"Maybe we will," Regan said. "Right now we're taking things one day at a time."

"Catch those two, will you?"

"We're certainly trying," Jack said with a smile as he and Regan stood. "We'll listen to the rest of the interview in the car. It's been a long day, and we still have an hour's drive to Hennessy Castle."

It was eleven-thirty when Regan and Jack got in the car. Jack turned his cell phone back on. There was a message from Keith. "Let's hope this is something good," he said as he pressed in Keith's number.

Keith answered immediately, and he sounded excited.

"Keith, what's up?" Jack asked quickly.

"There's a good chance the jewel thieves from the Nanuet Mall are Jane and John Doe."

Jack listened as Keith relayed the story, emphasizing that the female thief had complimented the saleswoman on her makeup.

Jack's hand tightened around the phone. "She mentioned the saleswoman's makeup?"

"Yes. And the hairdresser I spoke with said Anna Hager's mother was living in upstate New York the last he knew. The couple who stole the necklace told the saleswoman they were buying the necklace for her mother. We're checking out every Hager in upstate New York. If we could just find Anna's mother and talk to her, it would help immensely. If Anna is a jewel thief, I bet her mother doesn't know it and will unwittingly supply us with information."

"That's great, Keith. We were just on Regan's cousin's radio show in Galway. We told people to be on the lookout for a guy with a strange laugh."

"I'm sure you'll get a few interesting calls."

"I hope we get *one* that does us some good." Jack hung up, turned to Regan, and repeated the information Keith had given him. "If Anna Hager is Jane Doe . . . can you imagine? If we could just get another break in the case, it might be enough."

"I know," Regan said quietly, thinking how much she wanted Jack to be the one to reel in the Does. She gazed out the window as they drove out of Galway. I hope they're still here, she thought. My Irish intuition tells me they are.

But where?

Down in the bathroom of the Does' remote cottage, Bobby was brushing his teeth. Dr. Sharkey's temporary cap fell out and landed in the sink.

"Anna!" Bobby screamed. "I don't care what you do! I'm going back to Los Angeles tomorrow!"

39

Sheila and Brian had been driving north from Galway for nearly an hour. It didn't seem possible, but the dark, winding road turned lonelier and darker with each passing minute. They were finally nearing Margaret's cottage.

"Now remember," Brian said. "You've got to scare Margaret and make it very clear that May Reilly won't be happy unless Margaret takes back those paintings from her friends and, most important, gives them to us."

"Should I mention our names?" Sheila asked as she pulled on the black wig and tied the white bonnet around her head.

"I wouldn't be quite that specific. Sound ghostly, but get your message across."

Brian slowed the car and pulled behind a stretch of overgrown bushes lining the side of the road. He shut off the lights. "This is good. No one can see the car from the road."

"It's pitch black," Sheila exclaimed. "I'm not going to bother with this gooey white makeup." She opened her lighted compact and applied the dark eyebrow pencil. "How do I look?" she asked.

"Perfectly terrible," Brian answered. "Now go."

"What do you mean go? You expect me to walk down to her cottage by myself?"

"It's not far at all. You're dressed like a ghost. They're used to ghosts around here, but if someone sees me wandering around, they'll call the cops."

Sheila got out of the car, threw the cape over her shoulders, and hurried off into the night.

A groggy but anxious Margaret was huddled under a blanket in her darkened cottage. Outside, the night was still and quiet. Inside, Margaret had tossed and turned for hours.

The afternoon nap she had taken had agitated her with nightmares about May Reilly, but it had rested her enough that she couldn't fall into a deep sleep when she finally went to bed.

Margaret had dreamt that May Reilly's ghost had wandered into the greenhouse studio and threw all her paintbrushes on the floor. Waking up in a sweat, Margaret swore to herself that she'd never paint again.

Now Margaret lay awake in the dark. Her mouth was sore. She wondered whether she should take the aspirin she'd left out on her nightstand. Why not? She leaned over, turned on the light, and reached for the two white tablets. Then she thought better of it and turned out the light. I don't really need medicine, she decided. She hated taking pills of any kind. A minute later she flicked the light back on, popped the aspirin in her mouth, took a gulp of water, turned off the light, and lay back down.

A loud rapping at her window almost sent her through the roof.

"Margaretttttttttttt," a ghostly woman's voice called from outside.

Margaret clutched her covers, too terrified to answer.

"Margarettttttt. . . . I . . . know . . . you're . . . there."

"What do you want?" Margaret shouted fearfully. "Who . . . who are you?"

"You . . . don't . . . know? It's . . . May."

"May Reilly?"

"Of . . . course. May . . . Reilly."

"You don't sound Irish."

"What? Maybe . . . it's . . . because . . . I'm . . . *dead*!" the voice said angrily but with a more pronounced Irish brogue.

"You sound Irish now!" Margaret cried out. "Are you mad at me about my paintings?"

"No . . . I . . . love . . . your . . . paintings. . . . But . . . get them back from your friends . . . right away."

"You love my paintings?" Margaret asked, sitting up.

"Yes. . . . I . . . want the world . . . to see my lace design on them. . . . Give the paintings to that American couple."

"Those two? They get on my nerves."

"Margarettttttt," May admonished her, "do . . . as . . . I say! You made a deal with them . . . You must keep it . . . Not like what the Hennessys did to me."

"You're right, May. I'm dreadfully sorry about your tablecloth."

"The . . . people . . . who . . . stole it . . . will . . . have—"

Margaret cowered as May started to bang angrily at the window.

"—*very bad luck.*"

Margaret jumped out of bed, ran to the window, and yanked the handle of the flimsy shade with such force that it came off the runner and fell to the floor. "May!" Margaret cried as she peered out the window.

But all Margaret could see was the darkness of the night.

Margaret turned and went running toward her front door. She pulled the door open and yelled, "May Reilly! May, where are you?" Not caring that she was barefoot and clad only in her flannel nightie, she ran around the side of the house to her bedroom window where the ghost's voice had come from. "May?" she called but there was no one there. "May! I wish I could see you!"

Her heart beating fast, Margaret ran back inside the house to the kitchen. Brian O'Shea's cell phone number was written on a pad next to the phone. She dialed it quickly.

Sitting in his car down the road, Brian answered the phone. "Hello," he said, making his voice sound sleepy.

"Brian!" Margaret shouted.

"Hello, Margaret. Is that tooth keeping you awake?" he asked sympathetically.

"Never mind my tooth! Be here at six in the morning. We'll pick up the rest of the paintings, and you can have them! I have to get to work after that."

"Six?" Brian said jovially. "You're an early bird."

"So are my friends! Most of them have finished milking the cows by then. On second thought, make it five!"

"We'll be there, Margaret." He switched off the phone as a panting Sheila opened the car door and practically fell in. "You're hired!" Brian exulted as he gave Sheila a congratulatory hug, similar to the ones he had given his teammates on the football field after a good play. "She already called. We're picking Margaret up at five A.M."

"That's good," Sheila said, trying to catch her breath. "At first she didn't think I sounded Irish enough."

Brian laughed heartily. "Whatever you did, it worked." He turned the key in the ignition. Nothing happened. He tried it again.

The car was dead.

40

When Regan and Jack were about to turn into Hennessy Castle, they spotted a couple coming on foot from the other direction.

"Is that Sheila and Brian?" Regan asked, astonishment in her voice.

"I think it is."

"What are they doing out here now?"

"Who knows?" Jack tooted the horn softly and drove past the hotel entrance toward the O'Sheas. "I'll see if they want a ride. Hennessy Castle's driveway is a half-mile long."

As they pulled up to the modern-day Daniel Boones, Regan rolled down her window. "Fancy meeting you two again. Would you like a ride?"

Brian laughed. "No, thanks. We were just out for a walk—"

"A walk?" Regan laughed. "At this hour?"

"It's so quiet and peaceful. After the drive from Galway we figured it would be good to stretch our legs," Brian explained.

"We love long walks. We love to run. That's why we were in the Fun Run," Sheila said nervously.

"Walking is great exercise," Brian agreed with a half-hearted laugh. He tapped the roof of the car. "Thanks again for the offer. We'll see you back at the castle."

"Okay," Jack said. "I'll just turn the car around."

"You bet!" Brian said, tapping the car again.

Regan rolled up her window. "Why wouldn't they just wander around the grounds of Hennessy Castle?" she whispered.

"Maybe they're scared they'll run into May Reilly," Jack answered with a smirk as he did a three-point turn on the narrow road.

"Just as long as I don't."

The O'Sheas waved at Regan and Jack as their car pulled away and turned at the entrance to Hennessy Castle. As soon as the car disappeared from view, Brian and Sheila turned and ran back down the country road.

"Thank God!" they both cried at the same moment.

Margaret Raftery's painting, which they had removed from the trunk of their rental car, was lying on the side of the road wrapped in the black cape. Brian had tossed it aside when he saw a car approaching. If it had been the garda, he didn't want to have to explain why he was carrying the painting around at one in the morning. He certainly never expected to have to explain it to Jack Reilly.

"That was a close call," Sheila said. "Those two are everywhere."

"It's okay," Brian answered as he leaned over and picked up the painting. "We're still in business. And in a few more hours we'll be in the home stretch. By the time Dermot gets here, we'll be ready."

"What about making sure Dermot doesn't show anyone at the castle the paintings? We have to worry about Margaret and that manager Buckley. This painting was his."

"Figuring that out is my game plan for to-morrow," Brian said. "Right now I'm keeping my eye on the ball."

Regan and Jack were welcomed "home" to Hennessy Castle by a sleepy clerk at the front desk.

Twenty minutes later Sheila was wel-comed back. She made sure the coast was clear and then phoned Brian from their room. He was hiding in a grove of trees on the hotel's front lawn, clutching Margaret's painting which was still wrapped in the cape.

"You can come inside now," she told him.

And so it came to pass that in a second-floor wing of Hennessy Castle, just steps away from each other's rooms, the two young American Irish couples laid their weary heads on the castle's fluffy pillows. It had been a trying day for both the Reillys and the O'Sheas, but they were all hopeful about what the morning would bring.

The castle was quiet. The other guest rooms had been deserted.

Upstairs in the memorabilia room, May Reilly's plaque fell off the wall and crashed to the floor.

41

"Keith, I think we found Anna Hager's mother!" Tony Dufano shouted excitedly.

Keith jumped up from his desk and hurried to the outer room where several detectives' desks were clustered together. "What do you have?" he asked the intense young cop.

"A Sergeant Grick from a little town called Sweetsville is on hold. A woman named Hager who lives up there has a daughter named Anna."

"Put him through to my line." Keith strode back into his office and grabbed the phone. "Hello, Sergeant Grick," he said and then identified himself. "I understand you might have some helpful information."

A gruff chuckle came through the line. "I hope so. We have a woman named Hortense Hager who lives by herself in an old house on a big piece of property. She reminds me of the little old lady from Pasadena except on a snowmobile. Go, Granny, go. We've had to pull her out of ditches more than once, I can tell you that. We get so much snow up here, you wouldn't believe it. This winter was terrible. Hortense was in her glory."

Sounds like the same genes, Keith thought. "I understand she has a daughter named Anna?"

"Yup."

"What do you know about Anna?"

"Not much except that when we pulled Hortense out of a ditch last Christmas Eve, she said she was riding so fast because she was upset that she was all alone for the holiday. Her daughter, Anna, had called the night before to say she and her husband couldn't make it for Christmas. Hortense always has some excuse for why she's driving like a nut."

That was the night of the theft, Keith

realized—when the shoplifter had his teeth knocked out. "Her daughter's name is definitely Anna?" Keith asked.

"Yes. I remember because that was my dear mother's name, may she rest in peace."

"Of course," Keith said quietly. "Do you by any chance know if Hortense is home or away at this time?"

"No, but we'll find out for you. I know that once the snow melts, she gets bored and goes to Florida. But as I'm sure you heard, our snowfall broke all records this year. The ground is still covered, so Hortense may very well still be here."

"If she is, I'd like to talk to her as soon as possible. Where is Sweetsville?"

"We're just south of Rochester."

"Okay," Keith said. "Time is of the essence on this."

"I'll call Mrs. Hager right now and make up some inane question about her snowmobile. I'll call you back."

Keith gave the sergeant his direct number. When he hung up the phone, he looked at his watch. It was already after eight. When the phone rang again, he grabbed it like a hot potato. "Keith Waters."

"Keith, this is Sergeant Grick again."

"Yes, Sergeant."

"I called Hortense. Her answering machine picked up. She could be home and just not answering, so I'll have one of the patrol cars drive by her house. If there are any signs of life, I'll let you know."

been with each other every day, for better or for worse, in honesty and dishonesty, for eight years.

That idiot dentist! If only he'd done a decent job, she wouldn't be in this predicament.

Bobby had gone to bed.

Anna picked up their cell phone and called her mother. Perhaps hearing her voice might help. But she got the machine. "Mom, pick up if you're there. It's Anna Banana."

"Fancy hearing from you," Hortense said caustically. "To what do I owe this honor?"

"I just wanted to see how you were." Anna knew her mother was still mad about their canceled Christmas visit even though they had gone to her house in February after Bobby's teeth were fixed and stayed for a full week.

"Where are you now?" Hortense asked. "I can never keep track—"

"You know I can't tell you," Anna said. "Bobby's work is top secret."

"Of course. How is the dear boy?"

"He's not too happy. He had a cap fall out, and the local dentist where we are now isn't very good."

42

Anna was frantic. She didn't want Bobby to leave for Los Angeles without her, but she didn't want to miss her chance at the Claddagh rings.

She didn't know what to do. They had listened to Shane Magillicuddy ramble on about how wonderful the rings were, how any Irish man or woman—or anyone in the world, for that matter—would be thrilled to have one.

I know! Anna wanted to cry. I know! But Bobby was being so stubborn, and she was terrified that if they didn't stick together, something terrible might happen. They had

"When are you coming to Sweetsville?"

"I'm not sure."

"Someone's ringing the bell. I'd better go."

"I'll hold on," Anna offered.

"No, but call me tomorrow if you have any time." Hortense hung up the phone.

Anna stood there with the phone in her hand, not knowing what to do with herself. When in doubt, go online, she thought. She turned on her computer and pulled up every article she could find on the auction of the five Claddagh rings.

Shane Magillicuddy was a widower who lived alone in the house he had planned to sell. But now he wanted to keep the house. It was his lucky charm.

"I plan to enjoy these rings until the night of the auction," Shane crowed in one of the articles. "I hate to give them up, but I could use the money. And I'll have a grand time giving half of the auction proceeds to charity."

He must still have the rings in his possession, Anna thought. She looked up his address in the directory listing and a few minutes later was printing out directions to Magillicuddy's house. We'll take a ride up there right now, she decided. It's worth a shot. House break-ins are not our usual line of work, but Bobby certainly knows how to jimmy a lock.

"Bobby!" she called. "It's time to get up!"

43

"For he's a jolly good fellow," Dermot's friends sang as they shared a champagne toast on his luxurious private plane.

Dermot beamed. "I won't deny it!" He laughed and waved his glass in the air. "We're all jolly good fellows."

There were eight fellows in all, including Dermot and his assistant, Robert. Several hours earlier Dermot had told Robert to call his guests and tell them to get to the airport as soon as possible. "There are rings and paintings waiting for me in Ireland! I'd like to leave this minute!"

That was easy for Dermot to say. Robert

packed Dermot's bags and took care of all the arrangements. Dermot didn't have to lift a finger. The other six men, some of whom had to sweet-talk their wives into letting them go on this unexpected trip, were left to fend for themselves in the packing department.

But they all made it to the airport for the earlier departure.

"We're ready for takeoff," the pilot announced. "Please make sure your seat belts are fastened."

"Ireland, here we come!" Dermot cried. "We'll be at Hennessy Castle before noon tomorrow and then on the golf course immediately after lunch!" He settled back in his soft leather seat the size of a La-Z-Boy and smiled. He couldn't wait to see the expression on Brian O'Shea's face when he told him that he'd figured out what convent the nun who was, in his opinion, the next Georgia O'Keefe, lived in.

44

Bobby was not pleased when Anna woke him up.

"*Please*, Bobby, do this for me," she begged. "I have the feeling that these Claddagh rings will bring us luck. If we score them tonight, we can fly to Los Angeles tomorrow."

They both dressed in black and gathered the tools they thought they might need to break into Shane Magillicuddy's house: a hammer, a garden shovel, and a crowbar, among other useful items. They also had rope and tape that they would use to tie up and silence Shane Magillicuddy if need be.

It was three in the morning when they arrived in Salthill. The seaside resort on the north side of Galway Bay was very close to the ancient village of Claddagh where the famous rings originated.

Shane's old stone house was set back from the road, and mountains loomed behind it.

"This is lovely," Anna commented. "Maybe we should have bought a home around here."

"It's too close to Galway for us, but at least this street is isolated," Bobby said, licking his newly glued cap with his tongue. He had used the temporary cement that Sharkey had given him and had been shocked to see a red smiley face painted inside the cap. What a dope that dentist is, he thought.

"Anna, if you weren't so obsessed with those rings, I'd vote that this job was too dangerous."

"Shane Magillicuddy is old, frail, and lives by himself. You heard him on Reilly's show tonight. He's sweet and innocent. He probably doesn't even lock the door, never mind have a security system. This will be much easier than trying to steal the rings at the auction."

"Where are we going to park?"

"It looks as if there's an old shed down by the water," Anna said, pointing to her left, "Let's leave the car over there."

Bobby turned off the lights and steered the car to the side of the shed, out of view of Magillicuddy's house.

"Now remember, hon," Anna said quietly, "if we have to tie him up, let's be gentle. We just want to get the rings and get out fast."

"I know, sweetie, I know," Bobby said, still licking his cap. It felt as though it could be coming loose. "Let's get going."

The two black-clothed figures got out of the car and quietly closed the doors. With nimble steps they hurried across a field and around the back of Magillicuddy's house.

Bobby handed Anna their bag of burglar's supplies when they reached the back door, then leaned down to examine the lock. He turned to Anna and whispered, "These tinny little locks are a joke. I don't know why people bother with them." Reaching in his pocket, he pulled out a pin, picked the lock in two seconds, and slowly pushed the door open.

All was quiet in the kitchen.

He nodded to Anna and whispered, "Let's find the bedroom."

Stealthily they crossed the dark room, turned left, and started down a hallway.

With startling speed, a German shepherd bolted out of a back room and raced toward them, barking furiously. Terrified, Bobby and Anna turned to flee. Anna reached the back door, pulled it open, and ran outside, but the ferocious dog leaped up on Bobby's back, knocking him down. Bobby's face hit the floor, and his loose cap went skidding under the kitchen table.

"Tiger, what's the matter?" an elderly man's voice called out.

The dog turned away from Bobby for just an instant, giving Bobby a chance to scramble to his feet and make his escape. As he scampered toward the car, he could hear the dog racing around the house, barking his head off.

Anna, already in the driver's seat, was gripping the steering wheel tightly to steady her shaking hands. Bobby jumped inside, and they took off.

"Forget those rings!" he growled, licking the empty spot inside his mouth where Dr. Sharkey's cap had been.

"I know, I know," Anna said. "Listen, I was

so scared, I almost dropped our bag inside the house. Thank God I didn't."

"Well, don't rest too easy. My cap is somewhere on the kitchen floor!"

"Oh, no!" Anna cried.

"Oh, yes. We've got to get out of here on the first flight possible."

Wednesday, April 13th

45

Brian's eyes flew open. He immediately sensed something was very wrong. With great dread he turned his head toward the illuminated clock radio on the night table. It was 5:01! They were due at Margaret's house a minute ago! "Ohhhhhhhh!" he bellowed, flicking on the light.

Sheila stirred in her sleep. The dark eyebrow pencil that she had been too tired to wash off had smeared the pillowcase.

Brian shook her shoulder. "Sheila! Wake up!"

"Huh?"

"We overslept! This was not part of our game plan!"

Sheila's eyes fluttered open. "I thought you set the alarm."

"I did!" Brian leaned over and impatiently pushed the buttons on the black plastic clock radio. "Oh my God. I set it for 3:45 P.M.!"

Sheila jumped out of bed. "We'll get out of here in five minutes, but it's at least a half-hour walk!"

Brian picked up the phone and called the front desk. He hadn't wanted to order an early wake-up call because he thought it would arouse suspicion. He and Sheila had planned to wander casually past the desk at 4:15 A.M. with a camera and say they weren't sleepy and thought they'd take pictures of the wonderful grounds of Hennessy Castle as dawn broke. Now he sounded crazed as he asked the clerk how soon he could get a cab.

"Hold on."

Brian could hear the clerk talking to a cab company in an annoyingly nonurgent manner.

"Mr. O'Shea, that will be forty-five minutes."

"Forty-five minutes!"

"Yes, sir. Should I go ahead and place the order? We can bill it to your room."

"No! That's too long! Thank you." Brian hung up. "Wear your sneakers, Sheila!" he ordered. "We're going to run all the way to Margaret's."

"Call Margaret and tell her we'll be late," Sheila suggested as she rushed around the room.

"I'm afraid she might tell us to forget the whole thing."

They threw on clothes, brushed their teeth, and were out the door in a flash. In his frenzy Brian pulled the door so hard that it sounded as if it had been slammed shut.

Down the hall Regan woke up, startled by the loud noise. She heard a woman's voice admonishing, "Be careful!"

"I'm sorry!"

Sheila and Brian, she thought. Regan looked at the clock. It was 5:07. What in the world are they up to now?

46

After Keith got the call that Hortense Hager was home, he raced to La Guardia Airport and caught a ten o'clock flight to Rochester. A patrol car picked him up at the airport, and by midnight he was ringing Mrs. Hager's doorbell.

"I hope she's still up," Keith said to the young patrolman.

The patrolman laughed. "You don't have to worry. Hortense drives her snowmobile at all hours. We get complaints about the noise."

The door was pulled open by a wild-haired woman in her seventies wearing ratty snow pants and a sweatshirt. But her makeup was perfect.

Love the makeup, Keith thought. Please let this be a case of like mother, like daughter.

"Hello, Phil," the woman said. "I know I still have my snow pants on, but I put the snow-mobile away a couple of hours ago. The neighbors shouldn't be complaining."

"No, Mrs. Hager, that's not what we're here about. This gentleman needs to speak to you."

"Was there an accident?" she asked nervously. "I just spoke to my daughter a few hours ago . . . and my son sent me an e-mail this afternoon."

"No," Keith answered. "I'm with the NYPD," he said and showed her his badge. "I would like to ask you some questions about your daughter."

"About Anna?"

"Yes. May we come in?"

"I suppose I have to say yes," she said, her tone now feisty.

She knows this isn't a social call, Keith thought as they followed her inside to her den where a big-screen television was tuned to a cable news station. The embers of a fire were burning in the fireplace. The furniture was well worn but comfortable. The room had the feeling of a homey ski lodge.

"This is where I spend most of my time," she said as she pushed the remote button and turned off the television. "Have a seat and tell me what you want to know."

Keith and Phil sat on the afghan-covered couch. "Could you tell me where your daughter lives now and what she does for a living?"

Hortense sat on an overstuffed chair. "Anna lives all over. She is married and doesn't have to work."

Keith raised his eyebrows. "Sounds nice."

"I suppose. Her husband is a consultant. His job requires them to be on the go constantly."

You're not kidding, Keith thought. "Where is Anna now?" he asked.

Hortense paused. "I don't know."

"But didn't you say you just talked to her?"

"I did. But his job is—I know it sounds silly, but he doesn't like to disclose where they are. Someone could be tapping my phone, you know."

"It sounds as if his job could be dangerous," Keith suggested.

"I don't know. I really don't."

"Do you have a cell phone number where we could reach her?"

"No."

"So if there was an emergency, you couldn't get in touch with your own daughter?"

"She calls every week. Listen, if something happens to me or her brother, she'll know soon enough."

"Do you have an e-mail address for Anna?"

"No, I don't. If I need to leave her a message, I blog onto Sweetsville's message boards and make a comment. Anna knows that if I've left a message, she should call me. It's very easy."

"Could you tell me her husband's name?

"Bobby."

"And his last name?"

"Marston."

"Where did they meet?"

"In New York City. He moved into an apartment across the street from her in Greenwich Village. They bumped into each other in the corner deli, and the rest is history."

That's for sure, Keith thought. "So I guess he wasn't doing any of his top-secret consulting at that time?" he asked, trying to keep the sarcasm out of his voice. "I mean, he had an apartment then but he doesn't now?"

"What can I say?" Hortense spat. "They met, fell in love, and got married. He changed jobs. People do."

"What did he do then?"

"I can't remember."

"What about Anna?"

"She was a make-up artist. And a very good one!"

Keith's heart skipped a beat.

"Mrs. Hager, are you telling me that you can't get in touch with your daughter at this moment? You have no idea where in the world she is?"

"Listen to me! I'm not happy about it. She could be in the Witness Protection Program for all I know! I hardly get to see her. But she's still my daughter."

"What did she say on the phone tonight?" Keith asked.

"We didn't talk long. She told me that Bobby wasn't feeling well. The cap on his front tooth fell out—the kind of thing that normal people talk about. Nothing high drama. Then my doorbell rang, and I hung up. It was a policeman asking about my snowmobile. I now realize the visit was nothing but a phony excuse to see if I was here so they could bring you around."

"Mrs. Hager," Keith said, "we're interested in locating Anna, and I'm sure you are, too. If you had a picture of Anna and Bobby, it would help. I understand she called to cancel her visit last Christmas. Didn't that strike you as odd?"

Hortense Hager's eyes bore holes in Keith's. "Are you saying I wasn't a good mother? That she's acting this way because I didn't raise her right?"

"What? Not at all."

"If Anna's up to no good, it isn't my fault. I did my best. Now get out of my house! Get out! Out! I'm not giving you any pictures! If you're such a great detective, scout them out yourself, you Sherlock Holmes you!"

As Keith and Phil walked back to the patrol car, Keith was frustrated but satisfied. We'll get them, he thought. It's only a matter of time.

47

When Brian and Sheila came huffing and puffing on the road toward Margaret's house, they suddenly saw her car roaring down the driveway at a great rate of speed, kicking up dust and gravel. The car made a left turn and popped and stalled briefly before picking up speed again.

"Margaret!" Brian screamed, waving his arms and racing toward the disappearing jalopy.

"Margaret!" Sheila shrieked. "Margarettttttttttt! Stop!"

Their efforts to capture Margaret's attention were obviously successful. Her car skidded to a halt. A moment later it started chugging backward.

When the whining vehicle came to a halt next to Brian and Sheila, who were both holding their aching sides, sweating, and gasping for breath, Margaret rolled down her window and smiled. "Top of the morning to ya, lazybones."

The cap of her front tooth was gone.

Brian tried not to stare at the gaping hole in her mouth.

"You two look as if you modeled for my Fun Run decal, but you don't look like you're having much fun." Margaret started to cackle. "Get in the car before I take off without you again."

Brian and Sheila were not only amazed by the missing cap, which obviously didn't bother her, but by this new Margaret. Her lighthearted banter made Brian nervous. Better the devil you know, he thought. "Would you like me to drive?"

"No. You don't look as if you're in any shape to operate a vehicle at the moment. Now shake a leg! Punctuality obviously isn't your strong suit."

"We didn't get much sleep last night—" Brian started to explain as he hurried around the car and into the front seat. Sheila climbed in the back.

"You sounded dead to the world when I called you," Margaret retorted. "How much sleep do you need?"

"Oh, I was in a stupor," Brian insisted, realizing his gaffe. He wanted Margaret to think that he and Sheila were both unconscious while she was having a ghostly visit from May Reilly. "After your call I was just so worried that we wouldn't wake up in time."

"And you didn't," Margaret sniped as they tooled down the road. "Wait a minute—where's your car?"

"It broke down," Brian said sadly.

"When?"

"Last night in the very early evening."

"Why didn't you tell me that on the phone? I could have picked you up near Hennessy Castle."

"We figured that we'd take a nice early morning walk to your place. Exercise is so good for you," Brian said and then laughed. "We never knew we'd be getting such a workout, though. We had to run all the way over."

Oh, what a tangled web we weave when first we practice to deceive, Sheila thought as she rubbed her eyes and wiped the sweat from her forehead. She leaned forward. "Margaret, is there anywhere we could stop and get a bottle of water? I think I'm going to pass out."

Margaret turned her attention from the road briefly and glanced at Sheila. "What is that black smudge around your eyebrows?" she asked. "It's all over your forehead, too."

Sheila's heart almost stopped. "I don't know," she answered, thinking it was a good thing Margaret hadn't laid eyes on her last night in her ghost-of-May-Reilly getup.

Brian laughed, pulled a handkerchief from his pocket, and lovingly started to wipe his bride's forehead. "I know what that is. It's just a little black ink from our portable printer. Last night before we went to bed, Sheila changed the cartridge. That memorabilia business keeps us so busy! The ink must have gotten on her fingers, and then this morning we were in such a rush—"

"No matter how much of a rush you're in, you should always take the time to wash your hands," Margaret admonished. "Otherwise you spread your germs to other people."

Thanks, Brian, Sheila thought. Now Margaret thinks my personal hygiene habits are seriously lacking. "I did wash my hands this morning," Sheila insisted, "but once you get this ink on your hands, it is so hard to get off."

"I suppose," Margaret agreed. "It's like my paints. This morning I had to use turpentine to clean my hands."

"You were painting this morning?" Brian asked. "How wonderful. I'm so proud of you."

"Why should you be proud of me?" Margaret asked as she turned down a road that led to a lone farmhouse in the distance. "You don't even know me."

"I feel as if I know you," Brian said solicitously. "Like my aunt Eileen always used to say—"

"Sheila," Margaret interrupted, "don't you get sick of hearing about his aunt Eileen?"

"Margaret, you have no idea."

They all shared a laugh over the fictitious Aunt Eileen.

Margaret stopped and turned off the car in front of the quiet farmhouse. "I'm sure this will be quick," she said. "Farmer Fitzpatrick isn't the gabby sort when there's work to be done."

"I'm the same way," Brian said earnestly, "especially when I'm doing volunteer work. I get such satisfaction out of—"

"Brian," Sheila said, "enough!"

"You're right, honey. I should let Margaret get her work done. Farmer Fitzpatrick is a friend of yours?"

"Not really, but I try to be nice to him. His wife worked as a housekeeper at Hennessy Castle years ago. She was arrested for stealing cash from one of the guest rooms. They kept it quiet, but she hasn't left her house since. She's gone a little batty from the shame she feels. One unforgettable act of greed ruined her life."

Sheila and Brian mumbled their regrets.

Margaret started to get out of the car and then stopped. She pointed to a hose resting on the soggy ground near the side of the barn. "Help yourself to the water over there."

48

Shortly after the Does arrived home from their disastrous attempt to steal the Claddagh rings, Anna sat down at the computer and started searching for flights to Los Angeles. Bobby was furious. He insisted it was all her fault that now he didn't even have Dr. Sharkey's atrocious cap to cover his itty-bitty fang.

"I look like I belong in a Dracula movie!" he complained. "We should never have tried to break into Magillicuddy's house. I should never have let you talk me into it. It's not what we do! And because we wanted to ruin Jack Reilly's honeymoon, we stayed in Ireland instead of going to the charity event in Glasgow—after all the trouble we went to perfecting our Scottish accents! So what happens? Instead of scoring valuable jewelry, we end up with a tablecloth and a dental disaster. And I almost got killed by an attack dog!"

"But we did ruin Jack Reilly's honeymoon," Anna insisted. "He's running around Ireland looking for us instead of relaxing with his bride. Ten to one he won't berate us on the national news ever again."

"I don't care what he says, he'd better not find us," Bobby spat, grabbing May Reilly's tablecloth and tossing it across the room.

"He won't find us. He won't," Anna said as she continued tapping the keys of the computer. "Oh, good!" she finally cried. "Bobby, there are seats available on a flight tonight."

"Nothing earlier? I want to leave *now*. I want to get on a plane, close my eyes, and wake up in Los Angeles."

"All the daytime flights are full. I put us on a waiting list."

"I wish we could fly first class!" Bobby whined. But they had decided when they embarked on their life of crime that the less attention they received from flight attendants, the better. So they always sat in coach, usually in front of a kid who continually kicked their seats. "I'll go in and start packing," he said in a martyred tone.

Anna watched him disappear into the bedroom and then looked over at May Reilly's tablecloth that was in a heap on the floor. I should get rid of it, she told herself. If anyone came into the cottage while we're gone, it would be damning evidence against us. But then again, it could bring us so much money in the underground market. I'll figure it out later.

She turned back to her computer, booked their flight, and logged onto the Sweetsville blog to see if there was a posting from her mother. Usually after her mother was scrappy with her, as she was last night, she posted a message before going to bed.

Anna stared at the screen.

This time she hadn't.

Shrugging, Anna tried to shake off the uneasy feeling that came over her. I'll call Mom when we get to Los Angeles, she decided. If I call her now, Bobby will think I'm wasting time when I should be packing and closing up the house.

Anna looked at her watch. I shouldn't call

this late anyway. Stop feeling so anxious, she told herself. There's enough to worry about—like getting out of Ireland before Jack Reilly finds us. She fought off the urge to pick up the phone.

Across the Atlantic Ocean, Hortense was lying on the couch in her den. She had turned out all the lights after she threw out the cops. I should never have mentioned the Sweetsville blog to them, she realized. Now they'll be monitoring it for sure. And they've probably tapped my phone by now.

Anna, honey, don't call. Wherever you are, don't call.

49

Jack's cell phone rang on the table next to the bed. Although it wasn't even 6:00 A.M., he and Regan were awake, courtesy of their neighbors, the O'Sheas. "This *has got* to be good news," Jack said, reaching for it, "unlike most phone calls at this hour."

"Hello."

"Jack, it's Keith. I think what I'm going to tell you will make you happy."

"Try me," Jack said. He lay back down next to Regan, put the phone on loudspeaker, and held it between their heads.

"I'm in upstate New York, near Rochester, in a town called Sweetsville. I just had a chat with a woman named Hortense Hager who has a daughter named Anna. Anna travels with her husband, Bobby Marston, who is a—quote—consultant. Hortense said her daughter can't tell her where she lives or even where she is at any time because her husband's work is so top secret."

"It sure is top secret," Jack said sarcastically.

"My sentiments exactly. Anna was a makeup artist in New York City."

"She was?" Regan asked excitedly.

"Hi, Regan," Keith said. "Yes, she was."

"This is getting better and better."

"I know," Keith answered. "Anna met her husband, Bobby, eight years ago when he rented an apartment across the street from where she lived. Before she realized the reason for my visit, Hortense said she had spoken to Anna yesterday, and the most interesting thing Anna told her was that Bobby is having dental problems. One of his caps fell out. The security guard at the Nanuet Mall proudly told me that he knocked the teeth out of the guy who stole the necklace last December 23rd—which just happened to be the day the Does rented the P.O. box in Suffern and Anna called her mother to say she and Bobby suddenly couldn't make it for Christmas."

"You didn't ask Hortense if her son-in-law had a peculiar laugh, did you?" Jack asked.

Keith chuckled. "No. Hortense is pretty upset with me. She rather rudely threw me out of the house."

"Poor woman," Jack said. "She must realize Anna is up to no good."

"I'm sure she does. I called you this early because I knew you wanted to be updated."

"I certainly do," Jack agreed. "Never hesitate to call."

"I'll keep you posted, boss."

Jack snapped the cell phone shut. "Now we know, Mrs. Reilly, that John Doe has a loose cap."

Regan rested her head on Jack's shoulder. "And a funny laugh."

Jack sighed. "We're getting closer."

50

Sheila and Brian couldn't believe how well the morning was going. Four of Margaret's paintings were carefully piled in the back-seat next to Sheila and it was only 8:00 A.M. No one had quizzed Margaret too much about why the paintings had to be returned. She promised her friends she would paint them new ones.

"One more to go then—" Margaret began as she got back in the driver's seat.

"I thought it was two more," Brian said, try-ing to sound graciously confused.

"Let me finish, will you? I was about to say one more in these parts, and then we'll take a spin down to the gym in Galway. That will make six, plus the one you have from yesterday is seven. Then that's every painting I owe you. And I'm beginning to think you got yourselves quite a bargain."

Brian forced himself to laugh. "You're a card, Margaret, you really are. Hey, I thought the gym owner wouldn't give you back the paintings until you worked out a few times."

"I called him early this morning and told him I had to have the painting. I promised him I'd keep working out."

"Wonderful," Brian gushed.

"My paintings are good," Margaret said. "I just didn't believe in my talent. It's time I let it shine."

Just wait until we're out of town, Brian thought.

While they drove around collecting paintings, he figured out their next move. When they got back to Hennessy Castle, he would set up the paintings in his room for Dermot to admire and then give Dermot a letter from Sister saying how happy she was that Dermot appreciated her work, but she had a few more touch-ups to add before the nuns at her convent would pack the paintings in an extra-special religious box, seal it up, have the box blessed, and send it off to Phoenix.

Brian still had to write the letter. Dermot wouldn't arrive until until late afternoon. There was plenty of time.

And if Dermot insisted on taking the paintings back on his private plane, then Brian and Sheila would tell Dermot that only they could pick up the paintings at the convent and would, of course, deliver them to his plane. If Dermot has any decency, Brian thought, he'll give us a lift back to the States.

Whatever happened, the paintings could not stay at Hennessy Castle for the next five days—not with Neil and Margaret floating around the halls.

Margaret pulled up to the farmhouse where Brian and Sheila had had breakfast the day before. It felt like a lifetime ago.

I hope that kid with the camera doesn't come out, Brian thought nervously. That's all we need. "Last stop before Galway," he announced cheerily.

Margaret ignored him and got out of the car.

"Let's hope she doesn't stay for breakfast," Sheila muttered from the backseat.

"I'm worried about the kid."

"I know."

They waited anxiously. Ten minutes later Margaret came out with the painting. "I couldn't pass up a quick cup of Philomena's tea," she told them as she speedily backed out the car, her head turned toward the road.

Neither Brian nor Sheila thought it worth mentioning that Philomena's pajama-clad grandson had come tearing out of the house with his camera and was running after them.

When Margaret made it out to the street, she threw the car into forward and tore off down the road.

We're almost home free, Brian thought with relief. It had been a great idea to have Sheila dress as a ghost. Margaret was a different person, thanks to her midnight visitation. This morning she wasn't scared or hesitant. She was actually good company. Conversing with May Reilly's ghost had done her a world of good. The new Margaret will be painting, working out, and having a good time, Brian told himself. Her whole life will be different thanks to the influence of Sheila and Brian O'Shea.

In his wildest dreams he couldn't have imagined how different.

51

"Dermot and all you jolly good fellows, this is your captain speaking."

Dermot opened his eyes slowly, awakening with a heavy heart. He had been dreaming that he was back in his childhood home in Ireland with his parents. His family had been so poor. The realization that he was in his own private plane surrounded by his friends cheered him up slightly, but he missed his mother so much. He'd never found a woman like her.

"We have made unbelievably good time," the captain continued. "Strong tailwinds were in our favor. We're really flying, folks. We'll be touching down in another hour."

"That's grand!" Dermot cried as he looked around at his buddies who were yawning, stretching, and rubbing their eyes. "Coffee anyone?"

Mumbles of assent were heard throughout the cabin.

"Yes."

"Sure."

"Love some, as long as you're not making it, Dermot."

Dermot laughed and clapped his hands. "We'll have breakfast, get refreshed, and before you know it, we'll be out on the links."

"You're the man," Dermot's pal Josh said affectionately, giving Dermot's shoulder a quick pat as he stood and stretched his long legs.

Dermot looked up at his tall friend, a scratch golfer who had recently retired after a successful career as a stockbroker. "On this trip I'm finally going to beat you at a round of golf. I can feel it in my Irish bones!" Dermot said gleefully, his eyes twinkling.

Josh smiled. "No, you won't."

Dermot chuckled. Life was good. He turned and looked out the window. A blanket of clouds surrounded the plane. Back to my homeland, he thought. I should do this more often. I'm already enjoying myself. But the best part of this trip is going to be when I finally feast my eyes on those paintings.

And it won't be long now. We're way ahead of schedule.

52

Margaret scurried into the entrance of the Get in Shape gym. "Where's Coach?" she asked the receptionist, who looked positively bleary-eyed.

Clara, who had been up all night talking to Maebeth about her appearance on Gerard Reilly's radio show, feebly lifted her index finger and pointed. "That way."

Margaret barely noticed the grunting and groaning bodies in the workout room as she hurried past them to Rory's office. The moment he saw her appear in the doorway, he stood to greet her.

"Margaret, it's good to see you! Do you

have time for fifteen minutes on the tread-mill? Wait a minute: What happened to your tooth?"

"You sent me to a lousy dentist, that's what happened. Dr. Sharkey wasn't kidding when he called the cap he made temporary. He gave a whole new meaning to the word. The cap fell out as soon as I bit into a piece of buttered toast this morning. I can't worry about it now. I have other things to think about, such as my painting. I need to have it now, please. I promise I'll paint you a new one right away."

"I'm sorry, Margaret. Dr. Sharkey seemed like such a nice fella when he ran with his mother in the Fun Run."

"That doesn't make him a good dentist. Just because I'm a nice person doesn't mean I'm a good artist. But I am!"

Rory blinked. This wasn't the Margaret he knew. "You're a great painter. I told you that."

"I know you did. Now if you don't mind, I'll take my painting. I've got to get to work."

"Do you want me to call Dr. Sharkey and see if he can squeeze you in right now? Maybe he can do something to hold you over until—"

"Is that whiskey in your teacup?" Margaret

barked. "I wouldn't go back to him if every tooth in my head was about to fall out. Wait a second." She fished in the pocket of her gray uniform dress and pulled out the cap. "Take a look. Is this the worst-looking thing you've ever seen?"

Rory winced. "It's pretty bad."

"Thank you." Margaret put it back in her pocket. "Now I'll take my painting." She turned to face the wall where it hung. Shaking her head, she regarded her work of art with great admiration. Her initials in the bottom corner, MR, made Margaret's heart swell. She had always been secretly pleased that she and May Reilly had the same initials. She felt as though they were kindred spirits. But May Reilly got credit for her beautiful tablecloth. "You know something, Coach?" Margaret finally asked.

"What?"

"No more initials. From now on I'm signing Margaret Raftery to everything I paint, sketch, or scrub! I want to take credit for every bed I make, every table I polish—"

"That's the spirit!" Rory said encouragingly. "And you'll have more energy for all your activities if you work out at least three times a week."

Margaret grabbed the painting and, as though on wings, floated back out to the car.

"Done!" she said to the smiling O'Sheas. "The last of the seven paintings I promised." She rolled her eyes. "It was grand doing business with you. Next time you won't get them so cheap." She turned the key in the ignition and revved up her old jalopy.

"Last stop, Hennessy Castle!" Brian said joyfully.

"Our last stop," Sheila said from the backseat.

Somehow the words hung in the air.

53

Gerard Reilly arrived at work earlier than usual on Wednesday morning. He wanted to see if there had been any response to the appeal for listeners to call in about the Jane and John Doe case. But there hadn't been anything worthwhile. One listener, who obviously hadn't heard the whole show, reported that his neighbor laughed like a hyena. The neighbor was sixteen and lived with his parents.

Someone else called to say that there should be more laughter in the world, no matter what. The sound of laughter, however strange, reverberates through the universe and results in positive vibrations for everyone, she had explained.

Oh, goodness! Gerard thought. Get a grip. He sat at his desk and sighed. Regan and Jack were such a lovely couple. He knew how happy Nora and Luke were that Regan had found such a wonderful man. I would so much like to help them solve this case.

His phone rang. It was Shane Magillicuddy.

"Shane, it was grand having you on the show last night."

"Oh, I enjoyed it, Gerard. I certainly did. But listen to this. In the middle of the night, someone broke into my house."

"What?" Gerard said, sitting forward in his chair, his expression intense. "Are you all right?"

"I'm fine, thanks to my watchdog, Tiger. He's my guardian angel and my best friend. He ran after the intruder and chased him away."

"Oh, Shane, I'm so sorry. I hope it wasn't someone who heard you on the show last night and wanted to find the rings."

"Who knows? But don't worry about it. There was so much press about the rings before your show."

"Did you call the garda?"

"I did this morning when I realized the lock on the back door had been picked. Last night I didn't get out of bed when Tiger started barking and running around because I didn't hear anything unusual. And barking is what he likes to do best! I didn't even know I'd been broken into until I went into the kitchen a little while ago to make a cup of tea. The garda came right away. They just left."

"Did they find anything that might help them figure out who the intruder might be?"

Shane laughed. "Only one thing."

"What?"

"An ugly cap."

"A baseball cap?"

"No! A cap for someone's tooth. It was on the kitchen floor under the table. There were also a few tiny specks of blood. I couldn't see anything, but the garda certainly noticed them. What I did see was a cap that was really brutal. It even had a little red smiley face on the inside. Can you believe? I'm telling you, if I were the thief, I'd find myself a new dentist."

"Where is the cap now?"

"The officers put it in a plastic bag and took it with them. I certainly didn't want it."

"Shane, maybe you'd better put the rings in a safe deposit box until the auction. And maybe you shouldn't sleep at the house by yourself until then."

"I'm not alone! Tiger is protecting me. He'll watch over me and the rings. Anyway, I just wanted to thank you for having me on the show last night. It was a lot of fun! Say, you don't think that the thieves Regan and Jack Reilly were talking about could have done this, do you?"

"It's not the way they usually operate, but you can be sure I'll tell the Reillys."

"Good. I'll see you at the auction, Gerard?"

"Absolutely." Gerard hung up and immediately dialed Regan and Jack. A jewel thief is a jewel thief, he thought. I'm sure they'll be interested in hearing this.

54

Regan and Jack were enjoying a room service breakfast. They were shocked when they phoned downstairs to ask for coffee and were told that the chef at Hennessy Castle had one small stove to work with but would be happy to whip them up whatever they liked. A cart with eggs, bacon, juice, coffee, and bread was delivered to them in about twelve minutes.

"I love room service breakfast," Regan said as she took a bite of scrambled eggs. She and Jack were still in their robes, deciding the course of action they should take that day.

"I love room service with you."

Regan smiled. "The chef must be really bored. At the moment we're the only ones around to cook for." She lowered her voice. "What do you suppose Sheila and Brian are up to? There's something odd going on with them."

Jack was amused as he said, "Regan, you don't have to whisper. They're not going to hear you."

Regan laughed. "That's what my mother does even when she's talking about someone who's three thousand miles away. So answer my question. What do you think our neighbors Sheila and Brian are up to?"

Jack shrugged. "I don't know. But I wish they were our jewel thieves. It would make life easier."

"It sure would," Regan said, then frowned. "They were nice when we met them in the middle of the night outside, but then yesterday they bolted from the dining room when they saw us. They were walking around on a dark country road at one in the morning, and then they left again at five A.M. And she never dropped off the catalogue for her memorabilia business that she wanted us to have so we could order Reilly key chains.

They've been avoiding us ever since we told them we work in law enforcement—"

The ring of Jack's cell phone interrupted her. He and Regan looked at each other hopefully. Jack picked it up.

"Hello."

"Jack, it's Gerard." He sounded hurried.

"Hi, Gerard. I'll put you on speakerphone." Jack pressed the button.

"Hello, Gerard," Regan said.

"Hello to you both. Listen to this: I just got a call from Shane Magillicuddy. Someone broke into his house last night but was scared off by his watchdog."

"Is Shane all right?" Regan asked.

"He's fine. He didn't realize someone had been there until this morning when he saw that the lock on his door had been picked."

"I'll bet the would-be burglars were after the Claddagh rings," Jack said.

"That's what I think," Gerard answered. "Even though it doesn't sound like the work of the Does, I thought you'd be interested."

"Of course we are," Jack said, running his hand through his hair. "Do the garda have any leads?"

Gerard harrumphed. "You're not going to believe this one."

"What?"

"An ugly cap from someone's tooth was found on the kitchen floor."

Regan and Jack looked at each other in amazement.

"Gerard, my assistant in New York found out that the man we think is John Doe had a loose cap just yesterday!"

"Oh, Lord," Gerard said. "Well, it's supposed to look dreadful. Ugly as can be. It even has a red smiley face on the inside."

"John Doe has the money to go to a decent dentist," Regan said, "and it's never been reported that he has terrible dental work. We'll talk to the bellman here and see if he remembers anything distinctive about the guy's smile. But how many jewel thieves out there had loose caps yesterday?"

"Hopefully only one," Jack answered. "Gerard we'll come down to Galway. I'd like to go to Shane Magillicuddy's house and take a look around. I suppose the garda have the cap."

"They do. Call me when you're on your way, and I'll give you the directions to Shane's. I'll give him a shout and tell him to expect us."

"Thanks, Gerard."

Jack hung up. "Regan, can we be out of here in fifteen minutes?"

"Of course we can."

They showered, dressed, and were heading downstairs as Dermot Finnegan and his cohorts arrived in grand style at Hennessy Castle.

55

"Back to the grind," Margaret said as she turned down the driveway of Hennessy Castle.

"It's been so special spending time with you," Brian said. "And, believe me, your paintings are going to be so appreciated by our friends in America. Who knows? I bet we'll have people asking us for your number so they can get you to paint something just for them."

"Don't call us, we'll call you," Margaret retorted.

"Margaret, you kill me," Brian said with affection as Margaret parked her car in the employee lot. "If you don't mind giving us your keys, we'll come back out and get the paintings in a little while.

"Why don't you carry them in with you now? Just make sure Mr. Buckley doesn't see you with his painting."

"What if it started to rain?" Brian asked reasonably. "Thunderstorms around here come and go so quickly. We want to get a protective box so that not a single raindrop falls on any of your paintings."

"Whatever," Margaret answered. They got out of the car, and Margaret handed him the keys. "When you're finished, leave the keys under the front seat. It'd be better if Mr. Buckley doesn't know I had any business dealings with you. He might not like it."

Now she tells me, Brian thought. "I understand," he said sincerely. "It'll be our little secret."

"You two walk in ahead of me. Run along," Margaret instructed. "But don't forget to leave my keys."

Sheila and Brian held hands as they jauntily traversed the little bridge spanning the stream in front of Hennessy Castle. At the hotel's entrance, eight golf bags were leaning against the wall. Brian's stomach fell six feet. He held open the door of the castle for Sheila. "After you."

What transpired next felt to Brian as if it were happening in slow motion.

Dermot Finnegan and his entourage, all clad in blue blazers and khaki pants, were checking in at the reception desk. Sheila and Brian knew most of them. Regan and Jack Reilly were across the room, talking to Neil Buckley and a bellman.

"It's the O'Sheas," one of Dermot's group cried out. "Good to see you!"

Dermot turned around, his face filled with excitement. "Brian O'Shea, you are the devil! I can't wait to see the seven paintings I ordered! You're not going to believe it, but I figured out who the nun is that painted them!"

Margaret's voice cried out from behind the O'Sheas: "I'm not a nun!"

Everyone in the reception area stopped talking and stared.

Sheila and Brian were frozen in place.

"*You* painted the picture with the lace tablecloth?" Dermot asked Margaret, who walked toward him.

"I did indeed."

"And you're not Sister Mary Rose from the cloistered convent in Galway?"

"Since when does a nun wear a house-keeper's uniform? I'm not Sister Mary Rose, I am Margaret Raftery!" she said proudly.

"And Brian hired you to do the seven paintings?"

"He and his wife paid me one hundred euros for each painting."

Dermot's mouth dropped. "One hundred euros? I paid him half a million dollars to commission those paintings! He told me that most of the money was going to the convent."

"I can explain," Brian began.

"No, you can't!" Margaret cried. "You two are shameful! What you put me through. Thanks to running all over creation with you yesterday, gathering up my paintings, I broke my tooth and ended up with—" she reached into her pocket—"this dreadful cap! I've never seen anything like it! It's hideous! And you were cheating me out of so much money. Why you'd steal the sugar out of my tea!"

"I'll pay for any dentist you want . . . ," Brian offered.

"Margaret," Regan interrupted, as she and Jack hurried across the room. "May we see that cap?"

"Regan, why on earth would you want to see it?"

"It sounds crazy, but there's a chance it could lead us to May Reilly's tablecloth."

Margaret handed the cap to her. "Here!"

As everyone watched, Regan and Jack studied the inside of the cap. "There it is!" Regan cried. "It has a little smiley face in red ink. So did the cap found at Shane's house!"

"It's got what?" Margaret asked.

"Margaret, who was your dentist?"

"You don't want to go to him, Regan, believe me."

"Margaret, who is he?"

"Oh, Regan, I'm sorry. I don't know. I was bleeding and so upset—"

"Dr. Sharkey in Galway," Brian offered quickly. "We brought her there yesterday."

Jack turned to Neil and asked, "Can you get us Dr. Sharkey's number?"

"Right away!"

A moment later Jack was on the phone, hurriedly explaining to Mother Sharkey the reason for his call.

"My son puts caps on lots of people."

"May I speak to him?"

"Hold on."

Jack waited. No one in the reception area was moving a muscle. "Yes, Dr. Sharkey," Jack said and then identified himself. "We're looking for someone you might have made a cap for. . . . Yes, we did notice the little smiley face. . . . Uh-huh. . . . Great. . . . Well, we're trying to find a man who broke into a home last night. He lost his cap before getting away, and it had a little smiley face in it. . . . Yes, it was the home of the man with the Claddagh rings. . . . You heard about the break-in on the news. . . . You make a lot of those caps. Uh-huh. Any recently? . . . Two so far this week. We're looking for an American couple. The man has a peculiar laugh. . . . He was there yesterday?" Jack asked excitedly.

A collective gasp went around the reception area.

"But you don't know his name?" Jack grimaced.

Regan felt as if she had been punched in the stomach.

"Your Dad what? . . . He writes down your patients' license plate numbers because someone once left without paying."

Several people in the room covered their mouths, trying not to laugh.

"Yes, please, ask your dad."

Neil put a piece of paper in front of Jack and handed him a pen. After several agonizing minutes Jack started writing down a license plate number.

"We'll check this out immediately," Jack told Dr. Sharkey. "I can't thank you enough. We'll let you know what happens." Jack hung up and caught his breath. "Now I'll call the garda and ask them to trace the license plate." He called the number he had programmed on his cell phone.

A few minutes later Jack repeated what he had just learned. "The car is registered to a couple named Karen and Len Cortsman who live in a small town an hour south of Galway. From the address it appears that their home is in an isolated area."

"That's great, Jack," Regan said. "But it'll take us a couple of hours to get there."

"No, it won't!" Dermot cried. "The eight-seat helicopter I hired to take us to the golf course is on the lawn out back! It's all yours."

"I'm coming with you," Margaret cried. "If those two have May Reilly's tablecloth, they're going to answer to me."

Dermot looked at Margaret with admiration. There was something about her... "Then I'm coming, too!"

"Let's go!" Jack said.

"Brian and Sheila O'Shea, follow us!" Dermot ordered. "I'm not letting you out of my sight."

"I have a stake in this mess!" Neil exclaimed. "Martin, you're in charge while I'm gone."

Jack, Regan, Margaret, Dermot, Neil, and the mortified O'Sheas ran to the back lawn, boarded the luxurious chopper, and lifted into the air.

As they soared over the grounds of Hennessy Castle, Jack called the garda and alerted them. He then called Keith and said simply, "I think we're about to nail them."

The whole group was silent for the rest of the twenty-minute trip.

Please, Regan prayed, please let the Cortsmans be there. And let them be the Does.

As the chopper flew over green fields, the pilot gestured toward an isolated cottage. "That's the place you're looking for. We're going to touch down a little farther up the road, where the garda vehicles are waiting."

"Just a minute!" Jack said, looking down. "They're coming out of the house."

A man and woman looked up at the helicopter, hurried to their car, jumped in, and
took off.

That must be them, Regan thought. I can't
believe it.

"I think you may want to put this chopper
down and block our friends' escape," Jack
said.

"Gotcha." The pilot circled the property
and touched down at the end of the long
narrow driveway.

The couple jumped out of their car and
started to flee. Jack and Regan exited the
chopper first and ran after them. Jack caught
up with the male and tackled him to the
ground on the field in front of the cottage.
"Smile for me your pretty smile, Mr. Doe,"
Jack said tauntingly.

Regan tore after Anna who was unbelievably fast. Like a football player, Regan
lunged and managed to grab Anna's leg and
pull her down to the ground.

"Nice play, Regan!" Brian yelled enthusi-
astically as he caught up to them. "But this is
a team effort."

While Anna kicked and screamed, Brian
grabbed her arms, Regan sat on her legs,

and together they kept her on the ground as the sirens of the approaching garda vehicles grew louder.

Bobby started to scream. "This is all your fault, Anna. You got us into this mess."

"I wish I never met you," Anna shouted back at him. "I should have stuck to makeup!"

"It's here!" Margaret Raftery rejoiced as she came running out of the cottage holding May Reilly's tablecloth in the air, like a football player who has just scored the winning touchdown. Tears were streaming down her face. "May Reilly's tablecloth is safe and sound and on its way back to Hennessy Castle where it belongs."

Friday, April 15th

56

Regan and Jack had spent the last two days finally enjoying their honeymoon at Hennessy Castle—where things were back in full swing. Reservations were pouring in from people intrigued by the tale of the jewel thieves, May Reilly's tablecloth, and, of course, her ghost. And Shane Magillicuddy had decided that Hennessy Castle was where the auction of the Claddagh rings should take place.

"It will be a grand celebration of our Irish heritage—" Shane announced at a press conference, Tiger by his side—"to have May Reilly's exquisite lace tablecloth and Richard

Joyce's original Claddagh rings under the same roof for one night."

Tickets were sold out.

Regan, wearing the black silk dress she had worn to her rehearsal dinner exactly one week before, glanced out the bedroom window at the enormous white tent covering Hennessy Castle's back lawn. It was a beautiful spring night.

"This is going to be some party," she said as she gave herself a final spritz of perfume.

"You look beautiful, Regan Reilly Reilly," Jack said as he pulled on the jacket of his dark suit. "So rested and refreshed."

"I must be on my honeymoon."

Jack rolled his eyes and smiled. "Our honeymoon has taken a turn for the better these last couple of days. I bet Jane and John Doe wished they hadn't tried to interfere. *They* won't be living the life of Reilly for the next fifteen or twenty years." He extended his arm. "May I escort you, madame?"

"Why, of course."

They descended the stairs to the main floor and walked out to the festively decorated tent where guests were already mingling. Tables were covered with lace tablecloths and bouquets of flowers. Onstage a harpist was playing. May Reilly's tablecloth was on display in the center of the room in a new glass case.

Regan and Jack accepted glasses of champagne from a passing waiter and looked around the room. They said hello to the Sharkey family who were glowing with excitement.

Seamus Sharkey was thrilled to have been an integral part in an international police investigation. He had been on television and radio, and was written up in the newspapers. "All my work finally amounted to something," he said. "I'm ready to die now."

"Stop that talk!" his wife admonished. "We have a lot of living to do."

Seated in the corner, Linda and Brad Thompson were still behaving like newlyweds. She rested her head on her husband's shoulder, nibbled his ear, and stroked his back.

"How come you don't do that to me in public?" Jack asked Regan with a wry smile.

Regan laughed. "Somehow I don't think you'd want me to."

Dermot and Margaret appeared in the doorway, holding hands. Margaret looked elegant in a new silk pantsuit. She'd had her hair and makeup done at the spa in the castle courtesy of Neil Buckley and had obviously found a new dentist. Her smile was brilliant.

"I knew that whoever created that painting had to be special," a smitten Dermot had told her. "I feel as if I've known you all my life."

A still contrite Sheila and Brian were in their wake. Lucky for them that Dermot and Margaret had hit it off. It was the only reason they were somewhat forgiven. But Dermot wasn't going to let them off the hook completely. He had vehemently suggested that when they got back to Arizona, the O'Sheas spend at least ten hours every week for the next six months on community service projects.

"You were taking advantage of this wonderful talented lady," Dermot had chastised them.

"From now on, I want the respect you gave your aunt Eileen," Margaret added with a twinkle in her eyes.

Felicity, Neil Buckley's wife, floated by and said hello to Regan and Jack. She obviously had had a couple of glasses of champagne. "You haven't seen any ghosts around here, have you?" she asked them with a wink.

"What do you mean?" Regan asked.

"Let's just say I help Neil keep this place intriguing," she said as she floated off again.

Is she the woman I saw on the lawn? Regan wondered.

"Regan! Jack!"

They turned at the sound of Gerard's voice. He and Louise were standing at the entrance to the tent. "We have a little surprise for you," he said, then turned and called out, "Come on in. It's all right."

Looking sheepish, Luke and Nora appeared from around the corner.

"Mom! Dad!" Regan said when she saw them. She and Jack hurried over.

"We didn't want to interrupt your honeymoon," Nora explained, "but Dad thought it would be nice to bid on one of the Claddagh rings."

"*I* thought it would be nice?" Luke asked with amusement.

Nora ignored him. "We're staying with Gerard and promise we won't call or bother you. We just thought it would be fun to be at the auction . . . and then they moved it to where you're staying and—"

"Don't worry about it, Nora," Jack said. "We've been sharing our honeymoon with a lot worse!"

They all laughed.

Several hours later, after a delicious dinner, Irish music, and much merriment, the auctioneer cried out, "Let the bidding begin."

The Reillys—Regan, Jack, Luke, Nora, Gerard, and Louise, were all sitting together. And there was another Reilly in attendance as well . . . at least in spirit.